FINALE

CENTER STAGE BOOK THREE

REBECCA STONE

STARR STREET PUBLISHING

All rights reserved. No part of this book may be reproduced in any form or by any electronic means, including information storage and retrieval systems, without permission in writing from the author, except by a reviewer who may quote brief passages in review.

This is a work of fiction. Any resemblance to actual persons, living or dead, events, or locales is entirely coincidental. Any trademarks, service marks, product names, or named features are assumed to be the property of their respective owners, and are used only for reference. There is
no implied endorsement if any of these terms are used.

Copyright © 2020 by Rebecca Stone
All rights reserved.
Cover design by Rebecca Stone
ISBN

1

The crowd took their sweet time climbing out of the subway station, squeezing through the narrow stairwell to the outside world. Ella Davis wasn't even mad. After living in New York City for the past four months, the crowd's congested slowness meant being surrounded by all different types of people, all different types of stories. It meant being surrounded by possibility. She exited the station with a small smile on her face. The brisk March air held a warmer breeze than last week, and she made her way down the hill of Washington Street to the East River. Her mind drifted to Gideon, his broad shoulders and bright eyes while they'd walked along the river one chilly night in February, talking as lovers do.

After his bandmate Anthony got in a serious car accident in October, Gideon had to stay two hours north of the city in her small college town of Sugar Grove while his band, Eternal Youths, figured out what was next. Meanwhile, Ella and her business partner Rachel had moved their publicity company, Maven Media, to the Brooklyn neighborhood of Dumbo in November. Even though she and Gideon rotated visits to one another on weekends, she'd be lying if she said the distance wasn't getting to her. To them.

Or that the distance didn't help her tenuous relationship with her ex-celebrity mom, Margaret Davis, who got out of rehab in January and still lived near Sugar Grove.

Ella reached the bottom of the hill, couples and groups posing with selfie sticks and professional cameras. The spot was a popular tourist destination thanks to its location between the Brooklyn and Manhattan bridges, but it was also where she worked. The building that housed Maven Media was more modern than historical Dumbo suggested, the high-tech elevator leading to upwards of twenty concrete floors, each one housing a variety of offices.

She stepped onto the third floor, turning down a series of hallways to her office. Typing the security code on the bamboo wood door of the office, she entered and breathed in. She didn't know if she'd ever get used to the open space tucked away in one of New York's busiest neighborhoods. The white walls glowed with the sunlight streaming through the large windows that faced her, showing off both bridges and the river. A kitchenette stood on the right and three large desks sat on the left.

The soft rumble of subways echoed through the high ceilings, her heels clicking on the floors that matched the door as she made her way past the small lounge area to her desk. Rachel was at a meeting with one of their publishing clients while Julie, Ella's best friend and Maven Media's newly hired lawyer, was in the process of moving from Sugar Grove to the city. Julie had given unofficial legal advice while the company was finding its feet, but in February she had passed her BAR exam and officially joined the Maven Media team.

Ella sat down, turned on her computer, and checked her phone while waiting for it to boot up. Gideon had sent her a post-shower picture, his wet hair falling across his baby blues while drops of water sat on his muscular chest, dripping over his abs. She sighed, heat shooting through her core. She thought about the way his skin felt against hers, the way his strength held her both physically and emotionally. How even after sending a picture that made her want to take care of herself right then and there, he could then send one of him in his pajamas and ruffled hair, saying how much he missed her. She'd see him this weekend, but it never came fast enough. She needed his voice in her ear, his body above hers. He was her home.

Responding to his picture with what she hoped was a sexy office look, Ella signed into her email. Deleting the junk, she was left with contract follow-ups, press responses, and a potential new client. After the mishap last year when Ella almost lost their client Blue Bird Books — thanks to Gideon's ability to distract her — Ella and Rachel had further defined their roles in the company. With a focus on crisis management, Maven Media also dealt with traditional publicity: booking interviews, tour management, social media, and the like. They figured out by only hiring people with a background in crisis management, they could split the company into divisions. Rachel managed their two publishing house clients, Ella handled their four bands, and they were on the lookout to hire someone who could take over their three film and TV clients.

The email staring at her was for another band,

Flight of the Purple Birds. Based out of New Orleans, the mid-level indie rock band had heard of Maven Media from an old band client, Adam Driver Appreciation Club. ADAC had booked with a top label after the press Ella had done for them two years ago, and Flight of the Purple Birds wanted similar success. They had shows booked throughout New York City for the next month but their old publicist had left without warning. They wanted Ella on-site and to possibly tour with them, starting with a show in Brooklyn that weekend.

Ella read the email again. Their manager was willing to pay extra for the last-minute, on-site aspect of their needs. And of course her travel expenses. She tapped her fingers on the desk, knowing they needed to take the client but also knowing it would disrupt her life. She'd be unable to visit Gideon for the foreseeable future, but she wasn't sure he'd be able to visit her more than he'd been able to so far. Chewing her bottom lip, she leaned back in her chair. After Gideon's backslide into drinking over a year ago, she'd let him go to focus on her career. When he came back into the picture six months ago, sober and home from tour, she'd promised herself that if she let him back into her heart, she wouldn't make decisions because of him.

This was a decision she needed to make outside of him. They were together, and she knew that when push came to shove, he would be there.

2

Gideon Pike paced the same small section of floor and smiled down at his phone, the picture of Ella at a desk with her shirt unbuttoned more than was office-appropriate giving him something to think about. At least something more pleasant than the fate of Eternal Youths, the band he fronted.

"Hey, Gid. What're your thoughts?" Ryan's voice cut through his fantasy.

He looked up at their bassist leaning against the living room wall. "Sorry, what?"

"Jesus Christ," Anthony mumbled from his couch, his casted leg perched on the coffee table. Lucas, their drummer, sat beside him, staring at the floor.

"We were wondering what you thought about the replacement guitarist for the upcoming summer tour," Max said. The saxophonist sat in the armchair facing Gideon, his dark eyes tired. He'd joined the band unofficially in the fall for their first album, but officially joined in January once their label 4AD approved of the sax addition because they wanted the second album to have a similar sound. And now they had a new guitarist.

Anthony's alcohol-inspired head-on collision with a tree back in October had left him with a traumatic brain injury, a broken nose, and broken limbs. After multiple surgeries — including a couple to relieve the fluid in his brain — he was given the diagnosis of not being able to walk for a year. The cherry on top was a slight loss of coordination and an inability to play complicated guitar riffs. He'd moved back in with his dad and the band's manager, Tom, while they'd found a possible short-term replacement for the summer festival season.

Gideon sighed and pocketed his phone. "Guys, he's not great but we don't really have a choice." He looked at Tom, standing with his arms crossed and head down. "We've been through two replacements so far and we leave in two months."

"Gideon, he's only memorized one song and his playing is like listening to a fifty car pileup," Lucas said. "Maybe we could get different guest guitarists for each gig?"

Tom laughed. "That's not happening. I'm waiting for the finalized itinerary from Nate but by the look of things it's a solid five months on the road. Boston at the end of May followed by New York City, Tennessee, Colorado. A few weeks of road-tripping and relaxing our way to Chicago for two weeks, then a repeat of that on our way to San Fransisco before we make our way back to New York City for Electric Zoo at the end of August. If you'd like to find replacements for every show along the way, be my guest." He went into the kitchen, shaking his head, to start cleaning up the aftermath of delivered pizza.

The guys looked at one another. They knew festival season could be crazy, especially for newer bands that could play as many shows as they could get and didn't have the contractual obligations to headline only one or two festivals. Their label rep, Nate, had managed to get Eternal Youths on the radio with their first album release back in January, and the band had started to become nationally known. But eight festivals and a handful of small shows in-between was another monster.

Gideon chewed his lower lip, Ella steamrolling to the front of his mind. He had yet to buy a ring for her, but his plan was to still move to New York City and propose. Anthony's accident had set everything back. Gideon didn't see how to get the girl and how to tour with a booming band that lost its rhythm guitarist. He'd have to talk to his mom or his sponsor, Amy, about what they thought.

"This is a load of fucking bullshit. I can play, guys." Anthony's voice was mumbly, tired, his head supported by his hand. His forearm sported a long scar, a reminder of the bone that had pushed through from the accident.

"Dude, you can't even play 'Mary Had a Little Lamb.'" Ryan joined Tom in the kitchen, annoyance rolling off him in waves. Since the band formed in college, Gideon and his cousin Anthony had always been the partiers. They'd always been the ones that took things to the next level while Ryan and Lucas stayed straight. When Gideon went sober last June after their eight-month tour with the famous band The National, it left Anthony alone with his own devices. Despite having a heart-to-heart with Gideon about wanting to change, Anthony had still taken to the bottle. And now Eternal Youths was left to pick up the pieces. Again.

Gideon looked at his cousin staring at the ground. Trying to find compassion for the man struggling with demons Gideon knew all too well. He sighed, running his hand through his hair. Jack, their new guitarist, sucked. His playing was muddy, the chords running into each other like a train wreck. But he was sober, like Gideon and Max. Ryan and Lucas preferred to not drink, so sobriety was the more important need for the band. Even if it meant their songs didn't sound as good.

"I don't think there's anything we can do except maybe turn his amp down," Lucas said.

Max jumped in. "It'll be alright, guys. Seriously, we have three months. If we need to double down on rehearsals, we will."

"Works for me." Gideon was annoyed by the whole thing, disappointed in how things had turned out. Disappointed in Anthony the same way he'd been disappointed in himself not too long ago. But Ella helped keep him on track. She inspired their lyrics, she made him see light in the every day. And Gideon wanted to give her the life she deserved.

First thing's first: he needed to find the perfect ring.

3

Ella sat in the den of her apartment, her cat Pollack curled up beside her, staring at the laptop in her lap. The modern five bedroom apartment on the Upper West Side was huge, especially compared to what she was used to in Sugar Grove. It also cost a fortune, so everyday she sent a silent "thank you" to the universe for Rachel's dad being the CEO of a huge company and letting the girls of Maven Media move in — rent free — for the foreseeable future.

She'd hammered out the details with Rachel and Flight of the Purple Birds, her first on-site show that started tomorrow. They wanted pictures, videos, posted in real time. They wanted her to schmooze with the venue manager and the booking agent, the lighting guy and the sound engineer, and, of course, any backstage press that might be there for the headliner. They wanted her to make contacts for them, for future use.

When Ella had texted Gideon about being unable to visit him on weekends, he'd been supportive and offered to come to the show with her that weekend. She'd cleared it with Rachel and the band's manager; Saturday really couldn't come fast enough.

"Hey... girl!" Julie's voice rang down the hall from the front door, followed by a couple bumps and a small crash that sent Pollack running out of the room. Ella smiled and closed her laptop. Her best friend always made an entrance. The more dramatic, the better. Ella stood to investigate.

Julie leaned against the front door, panting, staring at the bags by her feet. Her blond hair was in a ponytail, her cheeks red.

"Hey, Jules. Is this the last of your stuff?" Ella picked up one of the duffel bags and pulled out the handle of a large suitcase, making her way to Julie's room.

Julie shuffled behind her. "Yeah... Finally... done. Whew." She sat on the unmade bed of what used to be a guest bedroom, taking a deep breath and huffing it out. "I need to go to the gym or something 'cause, like, wow."

Ella smiled, glad Julie had finally gotten all her stuff out of Sugar Grove and into their shared apartment. While Ella was used to living alone, there were worse roommates than her childhood best friend and her business partner. Ella grabbed the rest of the bags from the foyer, dropping them with a thud at the foot of the bed before laying beside Julie.

"You have a lot of shit."

Julie's laugh rang out as she fell back against the mattress. They stared up at the ceiling, laughing.

"That's what my mom says but hey, I got here, didn't I?"

"Yeah, it only took one car trip and a horrendous MTA excursion," Ella said, looking at her friend. Sometimes it was like looking in a mirror; they could've been sisters.

"So what's the plan tonight? This weekend?" Julie stood and stretched. "I need a shower, stat."

Ella sat up. "Well tonight I was going to stay in. We're signing a new band, Flight of the Purple Birds? I sent you the preliminary contract yesterday but I know you've been busy. They want me on-site for several New York City gigs and possibly a short national tour this fall. So tomorrow's my first show with them. Oh, and Gideon's coming over tomorrow."

Julie looked away, busying herself with unpacking. "How's... Anthony?"

"I'm not really sure. I think he's okay. I'll get the full update when I see Gideon. It's hard to get details over text when we only see each other once a week. If that." Ella felt her heart crack. All she wanted was to spend time with the love of her life. This was the second time Anthony had upset Gideon's life; the first time, he'd pushed Gideon to drink after two weeks of sobriety, and it forced Ella to make the difficult decision of letting him go. Ella thought about her mom, forgotten actress and alcoholic Margaret Davis. The consequences of her actions. How many lives she'd affected. She'd gotten out of rehab for the millionth time back in January, and so far it had stuck. The longest they'd ever made it post-rehab before zero drinks slipped into one which slid into three or more was six months — Ella wanted to wait before calling it successful.

"Well, I hope he's okay." Julie's voice was small, breaking the silence. She'd had a fling with Anthony almost two years ago that had started the same night Ella met Gideon. They'd mutually ended things after several months of fun, but routinely texted after. Julie rarely became attached to the guys she saw. After Anthony's accident, Julie had gotten a little more serious about life, a little more serious about her time. And she stopped dating quite as much.

Ella cocked her head, looking at her friend. "You okay, Jules?"

Julie stopped hanging her clothes in the closet. "Yeah. I just… I miss his friendship." Her voice cracked. "It's fine. I just hope he's okay." She went back to the hangers.

"You wanna do pizza and boxed wine and rom-coms?" The suggestion was standard for their biweekly Girl's Night, a night they'd started in college to make sure they saw each other. They'd included Rachel last year, but had fallen out of the habit between moving apartments and Julie's BAR exam.

Julie laughed and wiped her face before turning to face Ella. "Yes. Oh my *god*, yes. Jesus, why did it take us so long to suggest that? C'mon. I'm gonna shower, you order the food." She grabbed a pair of pajamas and closed the bathroom door while Ella went to the kitchen, opening the household Junk Drawer for the takeout menu selection. She grabbed the one for Chinese food, finishing the order as Julie got out of the shower. Ella grabbed the boxed wine from the liquor cabinet, pouring two healthy glasses so they could get started while they picked a movie and waited for the food.

After her time with Gideon had been disrupted by Anthony's accident and Maven's new client, after seeing the hurt Julie tried to keep hidden, Ella decided tonight was a night for self-care and letting go of the expectations they'd set for the people in their lives.

4

The venue was packed, and Gideon kept his hand on Ella's shoulder so he wouldn't lose her in the crowd. Her blonde hair reflected the colored show lights as she led the way to the backstage area, and he was hit with a wave of love for her. Gideon squeezed her shoulder, causing her to throw a smile at him before continuing on their journey. They'd come so far in the time they'd known each other, and seeing her be the boss she was filled him with pride. The fact she was his made him the luckiest man on the planet.

They eventually squeezed their way to the quartered-off section leading backstage, flashing their Press badges to get through security. The hallway to the green room was long, black, fairly empty. Gideon knew how this worked, knew that in twenty minutes when the opening band was done with their set, these narrow halls would be swarmed, the open doors letting in cold air while people moved equipment in and out.

Flight of the Purple Birds was hanging out on the beat-up couches pushed into one corner of the large waiting room, the opposite wall lined with a mini-fridge, snacks, and a couple of older men talking. The young band was waiting for their turn on stage, beer in each member's hand. Gideon stared at the bottles while Ella chatted with the guys. The alcohol musicians relied on helped ease the tension, helped them become the carefree people their fans loved to imagine they were. It helped them be fun. When Gideon had first started playing in front of people, he always had a beer and a shot beforehand. That had changed to beer during rehearsals, whiskey tumblers before shows. Shots after, to celebrate. Only to celebrate.

But there was always a lot of celebrating to be had.

"On in ten!" a stagehand shouted into the room before running past.

Gideon tried to pick up where in the conversation Ella and the band were. Ella was laughing about something, her face glowing. He smiled, never wanting to look away.

"You're also going to be at Electric Zoo, right?" She looked at him, setting her hand on his bicep. He'd always loved her touch, at once gentle but firm. Solid, as if to say she wasn't going anywhere.

Gideon looked between her and the band, realizing they'd been talking about upcoming tours. "Uh, yeah. End of August, but we're touring from May until then." He looked at the bottles again, feeling the familiar twang of craving the hoppy taste within. The ease of anxiety they provided. He looked around, spotting a single Coke on top of the mini-fridge, sandwiched between the two men. Anything to keep his hands busy.

"He's the frontman for Eternal Youths," Ella said, glancing at where Gideon's attention lay before turning back to the band with a smile. "They're with 4AD, they released their first album in January and are on the festival circuit this summer." She rubbed his back, nudging him in the direction of the soda. Gideon kissed her head before excusing himself from the conversation.

"Sorry," he said, reaching between the two men to grab his new drink of choice.

"No worries," one of them said. He was stout, his pie-face sporting a silver circle beard and ice-blue eyes. "How do you know these guys?" He threw a nod to the band, taking a swig from his drink.

Gideon was still working through the anxiety of social events without the aid of liquid courage. He popped the tab on his can to buy himself time.

"My girlfriend's Ella Da — Thompson, she's doing publicity stuff for them." He'd almost forgotten Ella like to use her mom's maiden for work purposes, to further separate herself from her mother's public downfall. And the bitter custody battle between Margaret and her ex-husband, actor James Berry.

Things would be so much easier once they finally got married and Ella took his last name.

"Ah, gotchya. Yeah, she's a doll. I'm their tour manager, Everett Sato. I found her through another band, Adam Driver Appreciation Club? They go by ADAC," Everett said, curling his jet black hair behind his ears.

"Oh, yeah. She helped get them signed with Matador, right?" Gideon drank his soda, looking between the two.

"Yep. We figured she'd know how to take these guys to the next level. You know a lot about the industry?" Everett's friend eyed Gideon over his beer.

Gideon shifted, taking another sip of the life-saving Coke. "Yeah, I'm actually part of Eternal Youths." Admitting who he was, speaking the name of a band that was quickly rising in the ranks of fame and popularity, used to fill him with a sense of pride. Not because it was a huge accomplishment, but because it made him feel important. Special. Now it made him shift on his feet, awaiting the inevitable surprise that came with being associated with a popular band.

"Oh, shit. No way, didn't your lead guitarist get into a huge accident in the fall?" White Walker's hand dropped, his words putting Gideon in a state of shock.

That was not what he was expecting to hear.

"How do you know that?" Gideon felt his body tingle, aching to run from the conversation. He didn't want to talk about his cousin. He didn't want to talk about what was happening to Eternal Youths. He did want a cold glass with two fingers of amber elixir.

"I heard through the manager grapevine; I'm their manager, Paul Adams. Yours is Tom Russo, right?" White Walker — Paul — was fully invested in the conversation, facing Gideon head on. Tom had, jokingly, always told the him and Anthony not to trust someone with two first names. The brightness of Paul's eyes was unsettling against his tan skin and didn't help convince Gideon otherwise.

He really did not want to be here.

Looking back at Ella, he saw the band stand to file out to the stage wings. Gideon managed to catch her eye and throw her what he hoped was a pleading look. He took another sip from his can and went back to the conversation with Paul and Everett.

"Yeah, Tom's our manager. We're prepping for a five month summer festival tour now," Gideon said, trying to steer the conversation away from his family.

A hand trailed along his back and he breathed a sigh of relief, relaxing into the strength of it. Ella came up on his left, all smiles.

"Hey, guys. It's show time."

5

Ella held Gideon's hand as they walked from the subway to her apartment. The show had gone off without a hitch, and she'd been able to post from Flight of the Purple Birds' various social media accounts and make contacts with the venue staff and a couple smaller press members. The venue had a capacity of almost 2,000 people, making it one of the biggest in Brooklyn. She'd also managed to give her business card to the headlining band's manager, which would hopefully lead to a new client. But she couldn't stop thinking about the look on Gideon's face when he'd been talking to Paul and Everett.

He looked scared.

She knew that look. She'd seen it several times, when she'd seen his internal war raging on his face.

She'd seen the way he eyed the beer everyone was drinking, and then shifted his attention to a lone soda standing on the mini-fridge. Ella knew he'd always been pulled into wanting to drink but had so far stayed sober. She counted how long: almost eight months. But being twenty-six and having dealt with her alcoholic mom since she was fourteen made Ella a bit jaded on the subject of recovery, especially when the person in question was an almost famous musician about to go on a five month tour. And when he happened to be the only man she wanted to spend the rest of her life with.

They entered the building, saying goodnight to the concierge on their way across the marble floors to the gold elevators. Sometimes her new apartment felt like a hotel, but after her apartment in Sugar Grove with the sticky front door, sloping wood floors, and loud neighbors, Ella didn't mind the abundance of luxury.

"I'm going to snuggle you so hard, darlin'." Gideon's deep voice broke through her thoughts and she couldn't help but laugh. She loved how hard he was on the outside, all muscle and tattoos and a serious set to his face. But she loved even more how soft he was on the inside, how willing he was to snuggle her and cook for her and — the best — love her.

"I hope you do more than just snuggle me," Ella said, raising her eyebrows before leading the way down the tenth floor hallway to the apartment she shared with Rachel and Julie.

Ella turned the key, opening the door slowly. Last she checked the time, the early morning hour had made her cringe. And that had been when they'd gotten from Brooklyn into midtown Manhattan and were waiting for the subway transfer to go uptown. The apartment was dark, and Gideon quietly closed the door behind him while they took off their shoes and jackets in the foyer. Roommates were an adjustment, and they crept to her bedroom in the dark. The other bedroom doors were closed, but they were always closed. Ella never knew when someone was home unless they were in the kitchen, the living room, or the den.

She flipped on the light in her room, setting her bag down on the ground.

"It's weird, now that you have roommates," Gideon said, closing the door behind him. Ella started getting ready for bed, watching him do the same. He squatted beside his overnight bag, thighs stretching the seams of his black jeans. Digging through the bag, his shoulders pulled at his henley, his biceps rippling below the fabric. He stood, hands going to the hem.

"Wait," she said.

He froze, his gaze turning lustful. Ella padded towards him. She stopped when her body was pressed against his, fingers teasing his hands until they released the shirt. He was a good head taller than her, and she tilted her head to look at him. He licked his lips as she took her time lifting the shirt, her hands grazing his heated skin as she went over the hard planes of his muscles. His skin was smooth beneath her lips as she trailed hot kisses across his chest, her fingers undoing his jeans, her body aching to feel his cock.

Ella's hands found their prize, his hard length filling her hand. Gideon's mouth covered hers as he pushed her towards the bed, fueling the fire raging inside her. Her tongue swept his mouth, devouring him. She'd never get enough. Gideon lifted her, his strong arms carrying her the rest of the way to the bed. He set her down, taking off his pants before climbing on top of her. His erection nestled between her legs, pressing against her sensitive core.

"Gideon Pike, if I don't have you inside me right this instant I'm going to explode."

The words tumbled out as his fingers tangled in her hair. He broke their kiss, a wicked grin on his face.

"I think, darlin', that if I'm inside you, you're going to explode any way."

6

How Gideon still wasn't making Ella cry out in pleasure was beyond him. And needed to be rectified immediately.

His body was between her legs, spread wide to accommodate him. Gideon decided pulling her shirt off instead of pulling her hair was more important right now, and the lacy violet bra she was wearing only made him want her more. He nibbled his way along the plane of her stomach, peeling back the soft cups hiding her glorious breasts. Her erect nipples begged for his tongue, and he willingly obliged by sucking and licking one perfect rosebud while lightly pinching the other. Her increasing gasps called to his need to take her.

He pulled away from her chest and worked her pants off her luscious legs.

"Where are your scarves?"

Ella looked at him wide-eyed. "M-my scarves?"

Gideon felt the heat — the need — to be hip deep in her hot core, making her cry his name, rise through him. His hands trailed along her bare legs, teasing her wet opening, making her gasp and arch her back at the tease.

"Your scarves, darlin'. I'm going to have my way with you." He thrust two fingers into her, her name on his lips and her hands clutching his shoulders. He kept them deep inside her, pressing against her innermost sensitive spot while he waited for her to respond. Her mouth gaped open, breathing heavy, her grip on his skin becoming tighter. Gideon could feel her muscles clenching, getting ready to ride the wave of ecstasy he promised.

But not yet.

He smiled at her, stopping his movements and pulled his fingers from her. She fell back against the bed, and he licked her sweet honey off his hand.

"Where are they, Ella?"

She pointed to her dresser. "Second drawer."

Gideon hopped up, finding a few silky ones that would do the trick. He climbed on top of her, setting one leg on either side, and took her wrists to the white iron headboard. Hissing when Ella pulled his cock into her mouth, swirling her hot tongue around him. He looked down at the beautiful angel before him, wondering again how he got so lucky. She released him and smiled.

"Take a picture, it'll last longer."

"I will never stop taking pictures of you, Ella." She'd never know how much she meant to him. How she completed him. How he didn't want a future unless she was in it. But he could make her feel sexy and beautiful, loved and cherished.

He finished tying her arms above her head and stood beside the bed.

"You're so beautiful." Gideon pushed a lock of hair from her face. He loved seeing her soft skin, her ample curves. She glowed in the light cast from her bedside lamp, her smile warming him more than any sexual fantasy.

"What are you going to do to me, big boy?" She bit her lower lip, nodding to his stiff erection.

"I'm going to make you scream. I'm going to make you come. I'm going to make you mine."

"I'm already yours, Gideon." She said it softer, the 'I love you' hidden in his name.

He crawled back between her legs and hovered above her while nipping her body, covering the bites with his tongue. Feeling the buck of her hips and the arch of her back against his body. She wriggled beneath him, and Gideon wished he could run to the kitchen for an ice cube. To slide the cold water across her skin with his mouth.

But having roommates limited things. He pulled himself away from her and took a third silk scarf, holding it above her stomach. He waved the tip back and forth, watching her body tense, her skin erupt in goosebumps. Ella's gasps egged him on, and his fingers moved closer to her opening. He dropped the scarf on her skin, whipping it quickly off as he spread her petal lips and leaned into them. He inhaled deeply, her scent calling to him, the only nectar that could quench his thirst. He slid his tongue through her folds, enjoying the taste of sunshine inundating his mouth; she was deliciously wet. He lapped again, resting on her clit, teasing the sensitive bud until she cried out. Until she clenched her thighs around his head.

A cry for something bigger, deeper. More raw.

Gideon groaned, his tongue sweeping through her hot center one last time before he sat up. He took his throbbing hard on in his hand, stroking, taking in Ella spread before him. Her skin was warm, flushed. She looked at him from half-closed eyes, her body still writhing with need. She whimpered, trying to move her hips closer to him. He kissed her inner thighs before positioning the head of his cock at her opening, pressing ever so slightly. She gasped as he slid in, taking his time for her tight pussy to fit him, pushing until her felt her wall. She wrapped her legs around his hips.

"Please fuck me."

"As you wish."

He pulled out and thrust, causing her to cry out, dig her nails into his shoulders. She was warm, soft, wet, and he slid back out, driving into her faster. Harder. Ella gasped, pleaded, her pants mingling with his own as he brought them closer to the edge. Closer to finding the bliss only the other could offer.

He felt her climbing with him, felt her muscles tightening as he cries grew closer together. He felt the wave take over, call to him, the power of complete release as he joined her. The power of complete release as their souls merged, the knowledge that the woman beneath him was the only thing he ever needed in this life. As he knew, without a doubt, they'd never be without the other.

7

The heat against her cheek was a dream come true, one Ella was happy to wake up to. She shifted, pressing against the muscled body beside her, smiling into the dip between his pecs. She wanted this — and last night — forever.

"Good morning, beautiful." A soft kiss dropped on her forehead.

Ella pulled her face away to look at Gideon. His eyes were still closed, his breathing easy.

"Good morning, handsome." She lingered a kiss on his lips, his hand moving to her neck. She felt something else move against her thigh, and Ella nipped his lip before her own hands ventured beneath the covers. He hissed as her hand found his cock, stroking lazily. Gideon's eyes, dark with need, stared at her, jaw clenching with each caress.

"Last night was fun," Ella breathed against his lips. She loved feeling him grow in her hand, loved feeling the ripple of his muscles as he shifted around her, bringing them both waves of euphoria.

"We could... do a quickie," he whispered, his eyes clenching as she moved faster.

"Mmmm, we —"

"Hey, Ella?" Julie's voice was muffled through the closed door.

Gideon's eyes flew open, Ella's hand stopping.

"Hang on, don't come in." Ella rolled her eyes.

Gideon laughed. "Goddamnit."

Ella tried to find a pair of pajamas to throw on. Gideon's naked form glowed in the morning light while he did the same, and Ella was even more upset their time had been interrupted. She knew he had to head back upstate today but until then, she wanted to spend every second wrapped around him.

When they were presentable, she opened the door. Julie leaned against the door jamb, inspecting her nails, dressed and ready to impress.

"Damn, Jules, where are you going? It's Sunday morning and I *know* you don't go to church."

Julie laughed. "Rachel invited us to family brunch in the West Village. Guess you're not going?" She wiggled her eyebrows, looking over Ella's choice in pajamas. Ella turned, Gideon quickly raising a hand.

"Hey, Gideon," Julie said, sighing before looking back at Ella. "I see you have company. Maybe next weekend?"

"I'm sorry, definitely next weekend. The new band client has me working shows at night so we didn't get in until late. Not sure when we're gonna see each other next." Ella felt herself frown, the reality of her split life hitting her; she couldn't spend time with her best friends or her man.

"Fine, I get it. Hey, Gideon? Tell Anthony hi for me." Ella stared after Julie as she headed down the hall, throwing on her jacket before shutting the front door with a thud.

Ella closed her door and turned to Gideon, who was already shirtless and sprawled under the covers. She smiled, shaking her head head as she crawled in beside him.

"What's her problem?" Gideon asked, scooting down so his eyes were level with Ella's. His hand went to her cheek and brushed the hair from her eyes.

"No idea, she's been in a bit of a funk. I think the moving thing isn't helping." Ella sighed. "When do you have to leave today?"

Gideon kissed her. "Soon. I promised my mom I'd stop by. I haven't seen her in awhile."

"That'll be nice, I'm sure she misses you." Ella pulled back, aware that she also probably wouldn't see him in awhile. She took a deep breath. They'd had harder conversations than when they'd be seeing each other next.

"When... when will you be able to come down again?" she asked.

His shoulders dropped with the question while he ran his hand through his hair.

"I don't really know, Ella. I'm sorry, I just... The new guitarist — Jack — isn't great so we're probably going to double down on rehearsals soon. I might be able to figure something out during the week, but I don't want to mess up your work schedule."

She knew asking him to visit her every week was a lot, between train tickets and delays and her own work schedule, let alone everything he was dealing with. But they weren't even supposed to be in this position; he was supposed to have moved to the city months ago. Ella chewed her lower lip, knowing now was probably not the time to bring it up but being unable to stop herself.

"I know we're both busy, I just want to see you. I know you were supposed to have moved here by now…" She rested her hand on his arm but quickly withdrew it at the look in his eyes.

He was the calm before the storm, eyes turning steely as they stared into hers. They stewed in silence before he sat up and started getting dressed.

"Seriously, Ella? You know you're the one I want, the only woman I want to spend the rest of my life with. You know I'll do whatever it takes to see you," he said, his voice low while he kept his back to her. "My cousin got into a serious car accident. Aside from that affecting the band's plans for literally everything, he's my family. I have to be there for him. Surely you understand that, given your mom." He stood, shoving his legs into jeans.

Ella felt herself tense. She didn't like talking about her mom, and she especially didn't like him using her as a way to justify his change in plans. She sat up, taking her time to respond.

"Gideon. I understand, but I also know you're going to be gone for five months soon. If there's a chance I'll only see you twice before then, I'd like to know, since it's my life, too. You're the only one I want but I'm trying to make it easier than it is, and you being up in Sugar Grove isn't helping. I feel like my life's moving forward down here and I just want to share it with you.

He turned to face her, hands clenching and unclenching, his eyes wet.

"Have you ever thought maybe I was in the same boat? Like my life is going one way and yours isn't? That whatever way it goes, you belong beside me? Ella," he swallowed and looked away. "I'm trying, okay? I don't know when it'll fit in with the band or the tour, but I promise you we'll figure it out. I know I need to move, but I also didn't expect you to move so quickly. You were basically given three weeks, and if the accident hadn't happened when it did I'd be here. We'd be here, together. But that's not what happened and now we have to roll with it."

Gideon turned back to her, grabbing his shirt from the floor and throwing it on, pacing the room. Ella watched him, trying to sort out what he'd said. She knew she was just scared. They hadn't had good luck with distance in the past. She watched him move, running his hand through his hair, and realized he was probably as scared as she was. Ella softened. The relationship she wanted — the relationship they had — was full of love. That's what they needed right now. She stood in front of him, placing her hands on either side of his face.

"Honey. I'm sorry, you're right. We will figure it out. I'm just scared about how it'll turn out, but I love you and you love me and that's enough." She scattered kisses across his cheeks, eventually landing on his lips. His soft lips, opening to her the way his heart had.

Gideon pulled away and rested his forehead against hers.

"It's always enough."

8

Amelia Pike scurried about her small kitchen, grabbing a stack of tea boxes in one hand while she held the lemon and honey in the other. Gideon forgot how much he missed the beautiful chaos of his mom's energy. How much he really loved her. They'd started regularly speaking on the phone once he went sober, but Gideon hadn't seen her in weeks. This time wasn't as awkward as their first meeting last year, when they hadn't seen each other in over two years.

He sat at the worn dining table, the same table they'd held family dinners at. The same table where they'd celebrated birthdays, where his parents had sat him down to tell him how sick his father was. The same table he and his mom would sit at while Tom would set down a homemade meal and clean the house. Gideon and his mom would stare at the food, silent crutches for one another.

Gideon watched his mom as he absently fingered one of the many scratches on the table's surface. He bet his name was still underneath, in the center, Sharpie'd on when he was six.

"Whew, here we are." His mom set a tea tray down in the center, her smile soft while she poured water from the pot into her delicate cup. "I wasn't sure what tea you liked so I brought a bunch."

He smiled at her, choosing an Earl Grey. Tea always made him think of Ella. When he tried to win her back after the tour last year, she'd had them meet at Tea and Me in Sugar Grove. The cottage set back on a hill served pastries and an assortment of unusual and fragrant teas. The owner, Maggie, was a friend of Ella's. Since Ella had moved to the city, Gideon tried to regularly stop in and check on Maggie. It didn't hurt that she usually gave him free desserts and tea to take home.

"How are you, monkey?" His mom's slight hand patted his much larger one, her pale skin soft and delicate.

"I'm okay, ma. I was seeing Ella this weekend, we went to a show last night." He sipped from his cup, looking her over. The wrinkles around her eyes were deeper than he remembered, her dark hair a little thinner, her cheeks not as rosy. But her gaze pierced him as sharply as ever; he'd gotten his eyes from her and looking into them was at once unsettling and comforting.

"Ah, the mysterious Ella. When do I finally get to meet this charming woman you're so fond of?" She winked over the rim of the cup, setting it down and grabbing a biscuit from the tray.

He smiled at her. "Not sure, we're running into a... scheduling snag." Gideon grabbed a biscuit and dunked it in the tea, happy to keep his mouth and hands busy for the time being. He knew he'd tell her about the brief argument that morning, but he wanted time to work up the courage. Once he'd gone into AA, he'd rekindled their relationship with weekly phone calls. While his sponsor, Amy, helped him with addiction, his mom had helped him learn how to forgive, and how to be grateful.

At the end of the day, she'd been his true saving grace.

"I know silence has so much to say and we should listen to it," she said, "but are you going to tell me what the snag is?"

"Yeah," Gideon said, sighing. "I was supposed to move to New York City last year, around the time she did. But I was going to talk to the band about it, and then the accident happened. I thought things were fine, but she got a new client that's having her work weekends. So she can't come visit me, but with the tour coming up and the shitty replacement guitarist, I don't know when I'll be able to visit her. She brought it up today and we got a little heated about it." He felt the tension release from his shoulders. He knew they'd get through it, but if being away from Ella didn't feel good, arguing with her felt even worse.

His mom nodded her head, looking past him. Gideon was hit with a feeling of sadness and wondered if it was hard for her to hear about his romantic life when she'd lost the love of her life almost twenty years ago and hadn't dated since.

"Hmmm." She sipped from her tea, setting the cup down gently. "I think it's perfectly understandable for both of you to feel the way you do. Distance is stressful. I think the biggest thing is making sure it's not infinite. You know I've always felt like you don't belong up in that town, but I know that's where the band is based out of. And I know Tom and Anthony seem pretty settled up there. Is moving even still on the table for you?"

"Ma, she's the one. I'm going to ask her to marry

me. I'd move across the world if it meant being with her."

His admission caused his mom to start, the shock visible across her features.

"You're going to ask a woman I've never met to marry you? You haven't been dating for very long —"

"Neither did you and dad." Gideon knew throwing his father into the mix probably wasn't the best move, and seeing the deflated look on her face confirmed it. "I'm sorry, I just... When you know, you know. Right? She's it. And she feels the same. So yes, I am going to move. I just don't know when."

"Okay." She stirred her tea, letting the silence hang over the table. Gideon wasn't sure how much time had passed before she spoke again.

"Well, Gideon, if that's how you feel, I would like to meet her. And soon, please. As for your snag..." She stopped to chew a biscuit, taking her time. "As for your snag, I think you need to come up with an end to the distance. Even if it's after the tour. Seven more months is doable. It sounds like she just wants to know what to expect, and I don't blame her. But I think post-tour makes the most sense. By the time you found an apartment and moved in, you'd only be spending time with her for a month before you had to head out. No sense paying New York City rent if you're not going to be here."

Gideon dunked another biscuit. She had a point, and Eternal Youth's last gig would be in the City anyway. He could stay with his mom while he found a place, and it'd be easier to see Ella. The band would have about a month to recuperate before starting work on the second album, and at that point it would be almost a year since Anthony's accident. Which meant his recovery would be almost complete and they could start fresh. And seven months *was* doable. It would be a shitty seven months, but at least there was an end date. If Ella's new client hadn't come up, it wouldn't even be much of an issue. Gideon didn't even know bands could pay for publicists to tour with them, but that's why they had a manager — that was Tom's area of expertise.

Gideon would have to ask him about it.

9

"Great, thanks so much for coming in," Ella said, standing. The interviewee stood as well, her curls bouncing as she shook Ella's hand and then Rachel's. Her tight pants and midriff top exposed more of her backside and belly as she put on her coat, and Ella couldn't help but wonder why so many of the people she and Rachel had interviewed showed up in outfits fit for going out. She didn't want to think the four years between twenty-two and twenty-six made such a big difference, but apparently they did.

When the girl left, Rachel made a face. Ella shook her head and smiled.

"That was... something. Did you count the number of times she said 'like'? I think my ears are bleeding." Rachel rolled her eyes, heading to the kitchenette to refill their coffee mugs. "But we really need to hire someone for film and TV. I received another email from B23 Productions and another from an agency."

Ella pulled out the folder holding the various candidates' resumes. They'd been sorted into yeses and maybes. After the candidates were interviewed, Rachel had written comments along the edges. Ella rifled through the yeses and pulled out her top three.

"I think these are our best candidates. They all have a background in publicity with an interest in crisis management. Two of them have minors in film studies and one has a minor in business management. Who are our clients again?"

Rachel sighed, setting Ella's mug beside her computer and taking a seat at her desk. "I have Blue Bird Books and Railway Publishing and am in the process of contracting Chastain Press. You have the bands Flight of the Purple Birds, Lo-Fi, Fire Forest, Strawberries, and Lolk Fore. I've been putting off BRICK Talent Agency until we hire someone but if we can sign them, B23 Productions, and World Talent, we could also possibly hire someone else to help your end of things. Having you on tour with bands complicates things, but we need the money. If you don't mind the traveling, of course."

"I actually love the traveling part. It's a little hard with Gideon also touring and not living in the same town, but if I can travel while he's touring, it'll be easier." Ella clicked on her Google Calendar tab to check the various tour dates, frowning at how many weekends she'd be missing with Gideon.

"Wait. Does Eternal Youths have a publicist?" Rachel's question caused Ella to freeze.

"I actually don't know." Ella swiveled to face her business partner. "I mean, they're signed with 4AD — one of the biggest labels around — so I'm sure they're using a company publicist."

"What if... what if we cold-called 4AD and looked into getting on some of their accounts?" Rachel leaned forward in her chair, resting her chin in her hands. "WAIT." She sat up, eyes wide and practically bouncing with excitement. "What if we asked Eternal Youths if they wanted to hire us at a discount so you could tour with them? Then they could bring you into 4AD and it's a win-win all around."

Ella stared at her friend. She hadn't thought about that, but it was definitely an idea.

"Wouldn't mixing business with pleasure be a

roll of the dice?" Ella bit her lip. On one hand, it could get them more clients through 4AD and she could travel with Gideon, which she also knew would help when he was tempted to slip into bad habits. But on the other hand, if any issues arose personally, they'd have to ensure it didn't cross over into business. And vice versa.

"I mean, it's up to you," Rachel said. "Something to think about, no?" She turned back to her computer and put in her headphones.

Ella looked at her a moment longer before swiveling back to her screen, unfocused while she mulled over the idea. She wasn't seeing Gideon for a couple weeks, and bringing it up on the phone didn't sound like a good plan. Especially after their last visit and that silly argument they had gotten into. Besides, she needed to really think about it. Chances were, 4AD already had assigned the band a publicist — their first album came out a couple of months ago, and they were going on tour in another two. If Eternal Youths were to bring in Maven Media, it would be too late for this tour.

She sighed, closing down her computer. Another problem for another day, when it wasn't 5 p.m. It was time for some takeout and pajamas.

10

The metal chairs were never comfortable, a reminder of why Gideon had started going to AA meetings every other Friday instead of once a week. He shifted in his seat, his long legs finding another position that would be comfortable for five minutes before needing to be changed again.

Amy, his sponsor, sat beside him, leaning forward with rapt attention. She genuinely enjoyed the meetings, tearing up at the appropriate times and always hugging those who'd let her. Gideon was grateful for her — her experience in the music industry as a sound engineer combined with being an open, loving member of AA had kept him on track. Especially for the first few months when he would call her at 3 a.m. and attend several meetings a week.

But now, Gideon felt good. Tonight marked eight months sober and, other than going up to share next, his head was clear. He still felt the occasional call to his vice, but it was nowhere near what it'd been. His friends didn't drink. Ella didn't drink around him. And Anthony not drinking or being at band practice since the accident meant his empty beer bottles no longer sat around. It was worse when Gideon was at a venue, when he remembered the ease it filled him with. He thought back to the show he'd gone to with her, how she'd known exactly what he'd been thinking. He hated talking about sobriety and she knew it, helping him subtly or by redirecting conversations.

"Hey, Pike, you gonna share?" Amy had leaned over, her face directly in front of his. Her hair was wrapped in a pretty scarf, glasses slipping down the bridge of her nose, displaying dark eyes and raised eyebrows.

Gideon sighed and raised his hand. "You know I'd rather not, but I know you want me to. And it's been eight months and I want my chip so I have to stand up anyway."

Joe, the meeting leader, called him to the front of the room. Gideon had thought over and over again about what he would say, but nothing seemed right.

He kept trying to find the words in his head as he made his way down the aisles to the center of the room. He turned to face the audience, fingering the copper chip marking seven months of sobriety in his pocket. Jesus Christ, he really hated this.

"So, um, yeah, I'm Gideon and I'm an alcoholic." The words still sounded foreign to him, no matter how many times they'd rolled off his tongue. But they sounded better than when he'd first started going to meetings, when he'd disassociated from the words he spoke in order to make it through. They sounded better than the denial he'd lived in for years before that.

But he still had to do everything in his power to not roll his eyes when everyone responded with the customary, "Hi, Gideon."

"Today marks eight months sober for me. It's been a long road and not an easy one. As some of you know, I work in the music industry and it's like… I'm surrounded by alcohol all the damn time. I work with my cousin and he would just leave his empty bottles everywhere during practice and I'd stare and stare. They always called to me until I threw them out." He took a deep breath. "I hated them, those bottles. But really I hated myself for wanting them so badly. Like I wasn't good enough, wasn't strong enough, wasn't… capable of being anyone other than who I had always been. I — I remember one of my bandmates last year randomly coming to see me at nine, ten in the morning. And he was surprised I was even awake." A scratchy sound escaped his throat, a laugh trying to hide tears. "And I realized no one really knew me outside of being drunk or hungover. And if they didn't know me, how could I know myself?"

Gideon swallowed the lump in his throat, staring at the ground. "Learning myself, knowing myself, is really what these last eight months have been about, and what the next eight months and the next months after that will be. I'm so grateful for the people that have supported me. I'm even more grateful to the people who have forgiven me and given me another chance. And that includes myself. I will forever be grateful I am here. Thanks." He kept his head down, taking his new red chip from Joe before heading back to his seat, trying to ignore the clapping. Falling into the empty space beside Amy, Gideon inspected the chip.

"I'm proud of you, Pike," Amy whispered, patting his knee. Her affectionate use of his last name brought him comfort, and gave her a small smile. He felt tired and was glad when Joe wrapped up the meeting, everyone jumping from the chairs to head to the refreshment table in the back. Gideon stood and stretched, grabbing his coat.

"Hey, Amy, I'm gonna head out. Thanks again, for everything." He gave her a quick hug and turned to head out before she could stop him with questions and conversation. He didn't always mind the chatting, but tonight wasn't that night.

11

Ella paced around the large island, passing the new stainless steel appliances of her apartment. Rachel's apartment. The subway tile backsplash was slick against the black granite counters but did nothing to distract her from knowing she needed to call her mom.

Margaret.

They hadn't spoken in over a few weeks, but last time they had, her mom had sounded good. Healthy. It'd only been three months since Margaret had gotten out of rehab. Only three to go before they hit their new all-time high of Longest Time Sober. Ella draped herself across the island, Pollack rubbing against her leg. No matter how many times she needed to check in on her mom, she always hated it. It'd been twelve years of her checking in, and Ella was tired. She wondered if she was always going to be checking in.

She just needed to do it, get it over with.

Waiting for her mom to pick up, Ella sat on the floor to better pet Pollack. He was unusually snuggly, rubbing against her hand before flopping to the floor for a belly pet.

"Hey, kid. How's the Big Apple?" Her mother's raspy voice was comforting, filling Ella with good memories.

"Hey, mom. It's good, busy. We signed a new client and they're paying for me to attend weekend shows and maybe to tour with them. How are you?"

Pollack started playing with Ella's fingers while she tickled his white belly.

"Oh, wow. Rachel must be happy, that's a big deal. How's she doing? How's this Gideon fella? Ya know, I still have to meet him."

Ella rolled her eyes. She knew the fact that Gideon was a musician would send her mom on a roll of what jackasses musicians were, how they weren't fit for anything more than fucking or friends. She also knew Margaret liked attention, especially since she wasn't a youthful beauty on the silver screen anymore. Spending all day with her could be exhausting.

"Rachel's good, also busy. She's managing our publishing clients. Gideon's fine. He's visiting next weekend." Ella definitely didn't want to go back to Sugar Grove anytime soon, and she doubted Margaret wanted to make the trip to the city.

"Oh, perfect. I can come down. I need to peek in on my agent, he's been strangely quiet the past few months."

"Mom... You were in rehab. Remember?" Ella stood, trying to walk off her annoyance. Her mom was always trying to play up being a victim.

"So? What does that have to do with anything? I make him money but he didn't even check in." Ella could hear Margaret getting heated, and she bit her tongue on pointing out how her mom hadn't booked a role — let alone an audition — in over a year. And how this was her millionth time in rehab and Richard, her agent, probably didn't hold his breath on it lasting. Ella sure didn't. She took a couple deep breaths instead.

"In any case, honey, would Friday work for you? I could catch up with you and Gideon after I meet with Richard."

Ella stared at the countertop, trying to hold onto her deep breaths despite the anxiety her mom stirred in her.

"I... I don't know, mom. I have to check the band schedule, they might have a show Friday."

"I could go with you to that! That'd be fun, a night out on the town together."

Ella closed her eyes. "Mom, that's not a good idea. Not only would I be at work, but Gideon might be there and I don't need my attention split between two people in my life and my client."

"Oh come on, you party pooper. You can work and I can get to know this man you've been hanging around for so long." Margaret's voice was getting firm. Ella had to push aside feeling like a child being chided by her parent. While Margaret would always be her mom, Ella was an adult and had learned the last couple of years how and when to build boundaries.

"No, mom. I'm sorry, but I'm not doing that. I'll let you know what day, but if you come down on Friday and I have to work, you could stay in the city Friday night and hang out with me and Gideon during the day Saturday. That's all I've got right now."

Margaret was silent on the other end. Ella swallowed her unnecessary apology, her plea to make her mom happy.

"Fine." Margaret let out a heavy sigh. "Let me know. Love you, kid."

"Love you too, mom."

Ella hung up the phone and picked up Pollack, holding him against her chest. He meowed in protest, wriggling to get out of her arms.

"Fine." She sounded like her mom, and Ella was hit with a sudden urge to answer emails, even though it was Sunday.

She would never be like her.

12

Gideon shut the car door, ambling up the hill to visit Anthony, who had moved back in with his dad after the accident. Tom lived in one of the small hamlets outside Sugar Grove, in an old house on over twenty acres. Close enough for Gideon to visit but far enough that he rarely did.

The porch was worn, the chairs weathered. Gideon rapped on the door and waited. When no one responded, he pounded with his fist.

"Jesus, I'm coming!" The voice was muffled but the choice of words gave Anthony away. There was a thud on the other end, followed by a crash, and the door flew open. Anthony leaned against the door, black hair askew and eyes half-closed.

"Gid? Man, it's early. What are you doing here?" Anthony rubbed his face and yawned.

It was oddly reminiscent of him looking hungover, and Gideon felt himself tense at the possibility of relapse.

"Dude, it's eleven in the morning." Gideon pushed his way past, glancing around the living room. He picked up a fallen picture frame and set it on the sideboard against the wall. The drawn shades made it difficult to really see anything. Gideon went into the kitchen, pulling back the curtains and grabbing a glass of water, the thump of Anthony's crutches following him. There were no empty bottles, no sour smells. Anthony took a seat at the island, head in his hands.

Gideon watched him. "How's it going, Ant?"

"Fine." He ran his hands through his hair, his shirtless body looking thin. Unhealthily so.

"Yeah? What've you been up to? You seem really out of it." Gideon set his glass down, taking a seat across from his cousin. Gideon had learned the hard way not to beat around the bush with him.

Anthony's head snapped up, a spark coming back to his eyes. "If you're insinuating what I think you're insinuating, then you can back the fuck off. I haven't had a drink in I don't even know how long and while I feel like I'm dying, there's nothing to even tempt me here. And I can't drive. So there's that."

Gideon eyed him. "Okay. I trust you." He felt like throwing up. He didn't trust Anthony, and something was off. "Where's Tom?"

Anthony rolled his eyes. "Grocery shopping. What are you doing here?"

"What, I can't check in on my bandmate? I just wanted to see how you were."

"I'm not your bandmate anymore." Anthony stood, thumping his way down the hall.

Gideon watched him leave before standing and checking the cupboards as quickly and quietly as he could. He wanted to believe Anthony was telling the truth, and the cupboards held no sign of alcohol. Of course they wouldn't. With Tom in the house Anthony would have to use a more discreet place, but it helped ease Gideon's anxiety to just check. Looking around the kitchen with his hands on his hips, he realized Anthony had been gone awhile and went to check.

The door to Anthony's bedroom was cracked open, and Gideon pushed it open. In the dark room, his cousin peered at him, sprawled on his bed with his arm on his forehead. A prescription bottle on his nightstand.

Pills.

"It was time for my pain meds and I have a headache. I'm gonna rest a bit."

Gideon nodded, the truth sinking in.

"Yeah, man, that sounds good. Let me know if you need anything." Gideon stood in the doorframe, waiting. Moments passed, and Gideon nodded his head before shutting the door behind him, his mind racing while he made his way home.

13

Ella set her phone on the counter, the speakerphone ringing while she dished her Chinese food. While she usually saved takeout for the weekend, it'd been a long week and it was only Wednesday.

"Hey, darlin'."

She smiled at Gideon's voice, at his nickname for her, a fire lighting in her heart.

"Hey, handsome. How's it going?"

He sighed. "It's going, I stopped in on Anthony yesterday."

The smile fell from her face. Based on his tone, something was wrong.

"Yeah? Tell me more, how was he?" She grabbed her phone and her loaded plate, curling up on the sectional in the living room and picking at her lo mein, feeling sick as Gideon told her what he'd seen. When he finished, she didn't know what to say.

"Ella? You there?"

"Oh, yeah," she said. "I'm really sorry, Gideon. Maybe it was just a bad day and not him taking extra medication?" She took a small bite of her spring roll, trying to swallow it while she waited for his response.

"I called Tom later. He had the same worry. Anthony is still on Oxy, but when Tom's not there, there's not really anything that can be done because Ant still needs his meds. Tom said he's been trying to calculate when the prescriptions need to be renewed, but he hasn't found anything unusual, like them needing to be refilled sooner than the intended date."

Ella stared at her food. She could feel the pain in Gideon's voice and wanted nothing more than to comfort him, to hold him in her arms while they figured out what could be done.

"I'm really sorry, Gideon. That's horrible. What are you guys going to do? Can I do anything to help?"

"Thanks, but no... Actually, has your mom ever gone through anything with pills? Given her history with addiction, and Anthony's, we're not really sure what to do."

Ah, next steps. She'd been there many times with her mom, although never with pills. Margaret preferred to drink, not get high. But whenever Ella had been in doubt, rehab had been the answer. She knew her mom would be carefully watched. Anthony needing his pain meds was a little different, but having round-the-clock care and doctors in charge of his pills could help. Ella sat up, setting her plate on the coffee table.

"I think you know the answer on what to do next." She released the breath she'd been holding. For all of Gideon's tough exterior, she knew he was soft inside. Admitting he needed help would always be easier than admitting there was nothing he could do for the people in his life. While Ella waited for his response, she matched her breathing to his. Any way to be closer to him.

Gideon cleared his throat. "You mean rehab, right?"

"Yeah. The doctors would be in charge of his meds, so at least he wouldn't be abusing them." Ella picked at one of her nails. "I know the last time he drank was the day of the accident, but if he's replaced that addiction with pain meds, then he's still hooked on something. And you guys had talked about him going to rehab before, right?"

"Yeah. But that was before the accident. Doesn't he need all the support he can get right now, while he's recovering?"

"Honey, it *is* all the support he can get right now." Ella sighed, her mind racing with thoughts of her mom through the years. "Believe me, I understand. But there are some things that are out of your control. This is one of them. Surrender. Let go. You're doing all you can for him. He's on his own journey, and he needs more help than support right now. You're supporting him by getting him the help he needs."

"Okay. I'll talk to Tom."

Ella closed her eyes, her heart hurting at the catch in his voice. "Good. Let me know what he says. But speaking of my mom…"

His laugh brought a smile to her face. "Oh, boy. Tell me more about your mom, darlin'. I love a good subject change."

"You might not like this one." Ella laughed. "She wants to meet you this weekend. She said she'll be in town Friday so I'm thinking you and I can grab lunch with her Saturday?" Ella picked at her General Tso's, enjoying the tangy sauce and lighter subject matter. She'd never had her mom meet a boyfriend before, but it sure beat talking about rehab.

"Wait... Seriously? Oh, shit." His laugh was nervous this time. "Well, it needed to happen sooner or later. My mom also wants to meet you, we could do that the next time I visit?"

Ella returned the nervous laughter. "Yeah, that sounds good. Guess there's no way around meeting the parents, right?"

"Nah, but you're the only woman I'd ever want to meet my mom."

The warmth spread through Ella's body. She really loved this man.

"Good, because you're the only man I'd ever want to meet mine. I can't wait for this weekend..." Ella shifted in her seat, clenching her thighs at the thought of him taking her over the edge, the way his muscular body felt against her softer one.

"You have no idea, Ella. What... What are you up to right now?"

She heard the suggestion in his voice. Her roommates were out and she didn't know when they'd be back. If they were going to have phone sex, now was the time. She headed to her bedroom, ready to do whatever he wanted.

14

The Lava Java was bustling, and Gideon looked around at students typing on laptops while tourists in town for the weekend admired the local art on the walls of the old brick building. While Gideon hated almost everything about the hipster coffee shop, he couldn't stop himself from coming here. Ella used to work here, back when she lived in Sugar Grove, but he'd never been able to visit her. Now visiting felt like a desperate attempt to have a piece of her, but he needed whatever he could get while they lived so far apart.

Gideon looked back at his computer screen, a slew of antique engagement rings staring back at him. He sighed, running his hands through his hair. Julie had helped him look for what style fit Ella the best, but they'd decided a vintage version was the best route. Since starting the hunt back in October, Gideon had found several perfect options at various estate sales, auction houses, and antique stores. Options that either were way out of his price range or rings he'd been outbid on, despite having saved almost all of his earnings from tour and using some of the money he'd earned when Eternal Youths had signed with their label.

A mug of black coffee was set down beside his computer, the force of the drop causing the hot liquid to splash onto his keyboard and the table.

"What the — " Gideon looked up, anger dissolving into annoyance. Ella's friend and old co-worker stood next him, arms crossed.

"I keep seeing you in here looking at rings," Ben said. "I know what that means and, while I'm not happy about it, I thought some coffee might help."

Gideon would never understood why Ella was friends with such an ass, but he did appreciate the coffee. He'd heard stories of Ben, but since formally meeting each other last year, Gideon had done everything he could to avoid the guy. The dislike was apparent on both sides.

"Thanks," Gideon said, trying to hide his irritation at wiping off his computer. Ben didn't leave.

"Can I help you?" Gideon asked. Okay, maybe

that wasn't as civil as it should've been, but he wanted the fucker to leave him alone.

Ben rolled his eyes. "I will never understand why she picked you. How's the search going?" He nodded towards the screen.

"It's going. Why?" Gideon looked at him, confused.

"Oh my god. Ella's one of my best friends, I just want to know she's getting what she deserves. And if she says yes, you know we're sort of a package deal, right? Which means it wouldn't hurt to be nice to one another." Ben stormed back behind the counter, banging pitchers and utensils while he cleaned.

Jesus Christ. Gideon didn't want to deal with a petulant child. But Ben had a point, and Gideon's current search for a perfect ring was turning up empty. He could try to make amends instead of searching for something he was beginning to feel didn't exist.

Grabbing the coffee, he sighed and ambled over to the empty counter beside the register. Ben was helping a couple customers, so Gideon stared at the vegan, gluten-free baked goods behind the viewing glass while he spun his cup.

"What do you want?" Ben asked. "I'm... sorry. You're right." He felt like spitting the words out. He could hear Ella in his head, telling him to relax and be kind. And Ben was one of her best friends, so Gideon had better get used to him.

Ben was visibly shocked, his face slowly molding into a smile. He nodded. "Thanks, man. I know we don't like each other, but we can be nice. For Ella."

Gideon nodded. "For Ella."

"So, tell me about this ring. Julie told me she'd helped you back in the fall but I guess you haven't found anything?"

That was the last thing Gideon wanted to hear. He hung his head, wrapping his mind around how the two people Ella loved more than him were also two people he couldn't stand.

"Yeah, we walked around one of the stores and figured out what cut, but all the vintage options I wanted haven't worked out. Kind of at a loss, but I want to ask her before tour."

"Tough break, man." Ben tapped his fingers against the glass. "I don't know what to tell you except to make sure whatever you do get, it's the right one. We both know what you put Ella through — the right ring is the least you can do."

Gideon felt fire roll through him, and he stood to his full height. "Hey, look. I'm fine trying to be friendly and shit, but at some point you need to let that go. I've served my term. She's forgiven me. I'm a different person and if you're not going to let me be that person, we shouldn't even try to be civil to each other. Is that clear?"

He felt better, telling the truth. Gideon was tired having the past held against him, especially by someone who didn't even know him.

Ben's shoulders fell. "I'm sorry. I just... Ella's like a younger sister to me. But you're right. I won't mention it again, and you won't act like that again." He held out his hand.

Gideon locked eyes with him, grasping Ben's offered apology with a firm shake.

"Deal."

15

On stage, Flight of the Purple Birds was rocking out, the crowd eating it up. Ella had been able to get some last-minute articles written up in some local e-zines before the concert, and they'd been able to sell out the show. She smiled from the sidelines, the band's manager Paul and the tour manager Everett clinking beers at the reception to the music.

"Well done, El," Paul said, raising his glass to her. "What do you say after this we discuss the future?"

Ella raised her seltzer back at him, smiling. "Absolutely, although I'll have to dip out around midnight." She stopped herself from looking around for Gideon, wishing he was there to celebrate the night's success with her. Eternal Youths had band practice into the night, so he was going to meet her after. A pang shot through her heart; another reality of them living apart. Ella turned back to the band, getting lost in their energy. They brought some of the jazz New Orleans was so well known for, but they offset the sultriness with dream pop.

She wasn't sure how much time had passed when the band starting shouting their thank-yous and moving offstage. Ella scooted aside while they passed her, high off the adrenaline that only performing a sold-out show could give them. They went to their managers, laughing and talking while waiting for the cries of "Encore!" to climax. Ella wrapped her arm around her middle, sipping her seltzer and taking in all the joy around her. She did wish the bubbly liquid with a splash of lime had something a little stronger in it, but she didn't want to kiss Gideon with alcohol on her breath.

Flight of the Purple Birds pushed past her to give the crowd what they wanted. Ella felt her phone vibrate as they launched into their first song.

On my way. Absolutely cannot wait to kiss you.

She smiled at the text, heat coursing through her body at the thought of what their kisses usually led to. Especially after last time.

Responding with something less vulgar than what she was thinking, she finished her seltzer as the band started their final song of the night. A tap on her shoulder caused her to turn around, and she met Paul's icy eyes.

"C'mon, let's head to the green room before everyone mobs it."

They passed Everett waiting for the band to come off stage, and Ella followed Paul's broad backside through the dark halls that became more crowded with stagehands ready to start breaking down the set.

Paul opened the green room door and closed it behind her. Ella took a seat on the sofa, one of the nicer ones she'd seen in a venue green room. She watched him pull a beer from the mini-fridge before sitting next to her.

"So, Ella. Tonight was a huge success, thank you." He smiled at her, clinking his can against hers.

"Of course, I'm so glad everything worked out." Ella sipped her drink, angling herself to face him more head on.

"Obviously we're thrilled with everything you've been able to do in the short amount of time we've been working with you. Not only are our booked dates starting to sell out, our online merch is as well. Not to mention our streams have jumped five hundred percent." He sipped his beer, his eyes never leaving hers. "We'd like to have you on our tour this fall. September to November, national only. Everything included, plus your standard pay and a travel bonus. We'll be playing everything from popular bars to colleges and small venues. We booked the shows, but we need your skills to get people to them and to interact with local media outlets."

Ella nodded, mulling over his words. It was a tremendous time commitment, but the money would be invaluable to Maven Media. She had no idea where she and Gideon would be at that point, especially since he would've just gotten back from tour himself. A Gideon-sized pit started settling in her stomach as she realized she could potentially not see him from May until November.

"I... Thank you, that's an incredibly generous offer. I will, of course, have to discuss it with Rachel." Ella drank from her can, knowing Rachel would want her to agree. Knowing Gideon would also want her to take it. She'd let him go for her career before. But she wasn't sure she wanted to do that again.

Despite the disappointment on his face, Paul nodded. "I understand. We'll need to book someone else if you're unable to. Would you be able to give us an answer by end of next week?"

"Of course." Ella's phone, wedged between her

and the couch, vibrated. "I'll try to let you know sooner. Unfortunately, though, I do have to take off." She stood, smiling, and shook his hand.

She had a hot date, and she wasn't going to miss it for the world.

16

Gideon bounced on the balls of his feet, trying to warm himself against the wind. People were streaming out of the venue, marking the end of a successful show.

"Hey, handsome."

His face broke into a shit-eating grin, the sound of his one and only making the brisk March air disappear. Ella bounded down the sidewalk and into his arms, wrapping herself around him like a koala bear. His adorable, funny, sweet, smart koala bear.

"Hey, darlin'. How was the show?" He managed to get the words out between kisses. He squeezed her against him until she was as close as possible, even though it'd never be close enough.

"It was fine, would've been better if you'd been there," Ella said, running her hands through his hair, resting her elbows on his shoulders while he carried her down the sidewalk. He took his time, enjoying the feel of her in his arms, her ass in his hands, the sunshine taste of her lips against his.

"Hmmm maybe next time." He kissed her, deeply, his tongue searching for her heart with every breath. She melted against him, her tongue tangling with his. The world around them disappeared, as it always did when he was with her.

She pulled away, smiling ear-to-ear. "I missed you. Can we take this someplace warmer? And maybe softer?" She waggled her eyebrows at the implication of a mattress as she slid down his body, biting her lip as she slid over his hard length that pulled his jeans tight.

"Damn, babe, not here!" he said.

She laughed, pulling him along to the subway. He would let her pull him anywhere, especially if it meant watching her from behind. Without heels, she was on the shorter side of things, her curves looking even more luscious. How she could pull off going from the sexiest woman he'd ever seen to the most beautiful and still to the cutest, Gideon would never know. They boarded the train, riding several stops in silence, taking in the late night members sharing the car.

"How's Anthony? How was band practice?" Her voice was almost drowned out by the screech of the stopping subway.

Gideon took a deep breath. He didn't exactly want to talk about his addicted cousin, but he also didn't want to talk about how terrible the band was with Jack. He especially didn't want to talk about how Jack being bad impacted Gideon's ability to visit her.

First things first.

"Ant's okay. I talked to Tom and we agreed rehab would be the best option, but I'm not sure how we're going to get it to happen. I think he needs a few days to think on it. And band practice..." He turned to look at Ella. "It's not good."

She looked at him, brow furrowed. "Like, in what way? Is it... is it bad?"

Gideon sighed, leaning forward. "Yeah, it's bad. So bad that Tom's calling practice every weekend until we leave for tour." He let the words hang between them before hazarding a glance at Ella. She just stared at him, her face blank.

"Every weekend." She leaned back against the bench, staring out the windows at the passing tunnel.

"Yeah, every weekend." Gideon leaned back with

her, his eyes never leaving her face. Ella let out a long breath.

"Okay... Okay. So. Every weekend. I... When will we see each other, Gideon?" She turned towards him. He'd never seen her scared. Her wet eyes — puppy eyes — nearly broke him. He swallowed his own emotions, trying not to betray how scared he felt as well.

"I don't know, Ella. We'll work it out, we always do." He reached for her hand, holding it between both of his. Memorizing the shape of her fingers, the warmth of her palm. "We'll enjoy tonight and worry about the next time when it's time to worry about it. Okay?" Raising her hand to his lips, he pressed a kiss against her skin, lingering. She'd always been his rock; it was his turn to be hers.

"Besides, we're going to have a fun weekend. What time are we meeting your mom?" Gideon thought changing the subject would be helpful, but the way Ella threw her head back and groaned said otherwise.

"Ugh, we're grabbing lunch around 1 p.m. in Midtown." She turned to face him. "This really sucks. Can you make it up to me this weekend?"

Gideon smiled, licking his lips. "Anything for

you. I've been thinking about what I want to do to you all week."

"Good, 'cause I have some of my own news to share."

The smile fell from Gideon's face as quickly as it had appeared. "What kind of news?"

"Flight of the Purple Birds wants me to tour with them September to November. National tour, they'll pay all expenses, our standard rate, and an on-site bonus. But I know you're touring May through August. So... Yeah." She looked forward. "C'mon, this is our stop."

Gideon followed her in a daze, what she'd said still ringing through his ears. If he couldn't visit her until September, and she couldn't visit him until November, where did that leave them?

17

They walked from Penn Station to Greeley Square in Midtown, Ella's fingers dancing in Gideon's hand. He eventually squeezed, an attempt to calm her nerves. Ella had stopped introducing friends to her mom once she hit double digits, but she'd never introduced a boyfriend.

The statue of Horace Greeley stared down at them while they waited, Ella scanning the crowd for Margaret. When she spotted her mom, Ella gave a wave and squeezed Gideon's hand, unable to move from her spot. Margaret came over. Despite years of drinking — and a few years of smoking — she was still pretty. More than that, she had an energy about her that people noticed. Ella had forgotten those things, or maybe she didn't always see them. She couldn't remember the last time she'd seen Margaret in public.

In her youth, her mom had been on the brink of becoming America's next sweetheart. The potential still showed in her smile, in the hop in her step, the way the crowd naturally parted, some faces turning, staring a moment too short for recognition but too long for comfort. Ella could gather what a couple like her and her father had made, two beautiful human beings with personalities that outshone everyone around them.

Margaret reached them and gave Ella a strong hug. Ella closed her eyes and leaned into it, immediately becoming a kid again.

Margaret pulled away, her hands resting on Ella's arms while she looked her over.

"Oh, I've missed you, honey." She ran a hand over Ella's hair, cupped her face, smiled. Turning to Gideon, her smile turned into a grin and she fluffed her hair.

"My, my, you must be the Gideon I've heard so much about. I'm Margaret, pleased to meet you." She held out her hand as if she expected him to kiss the top of it. Ella refrained from rolling her eyes at the inherent drama her mom possessed, and even more so when Gideon obliged.

"The pleasure is all mine," he said, releasing her mom's fingers.

Margaret looked between the two of them, her grin wiping almost twenty years from her face. Ella watched her carefully, but instead of finding any warning signs, she found the opposite. Her mom's skin glowed and her eyes were clear. She looked healthy.

"So kids, where are we going? I have all the time in the world for you." She moved between them, looping her arms through each of theirs and walking them down the street. A true non-city resident, Margaret's entitlement to taking up the entire sidewalk immediately drove Ella crazy, and she tried to make herself small against the oncoming stream of people.

"Mom, let's pull over here and figure out where we're going."

"What was that, honey?" Margaret's gravelly voice was almost lost in the noise of the city.

Ella sighed. "Can we stop for a minute and figure out where we're going?"

"We can do that while we walk!" Margaret laughed. "Let's soak in the city air while we can."

Gideon met Ella's eyes over the top of her head, and Ella tried not to let her frustration come through. She must not have done a good job of it because Gideon started directing them closer to the wall of a building.

"I need to get my bearings, Margaret. Sorry." He unlooped his arm from hers, pulling out his phone. "What is everyone in the mood for? This area is Koreatown but I'm sure we can find something else."

Ella leaned in to look at his screen, enjoying the feel of his arm against her cheek. She inhaled his warm scent, taking long, slow breaths to re-center herself. When she felt calm enough to deal with her mom, she looked up at Margaret, who winked at her. Ella rolled her eyes. She knew how attractive Gideon was, how he radiated a primal energy that made her want to stay in bed with him forever, how his rugged good looks were offset by his inherent ability to go from laughing to brooding. Ella just didn't need her mom making eyes at him.

"What do you think, mom?"

Margaret looked around. "There's a good Korean barbecue place around here, but I can't remember the name of it. I think it starts with a 'b'? I remember they have really great meat." Ella watched her mom catch herself from laughing at her own innuendo. Margaret was one of those people who laughed at her own jokes, even when no one else did. And the dirtier, the better.

"There's one called Baekjeong? It's a couple blocks from here," Gideon said.

"Yes!" Margaret practically jumped up and down. "That's the one. Lead the way, handsome."

Gideon smiled and grabbed Ella's hand, planting a quick kiss on her lips before they made their way to the restaurant. Ella held onto the small affection the entire way, wanting to run from this forced downtime with her boyfriend and erratic mom.

18

Gideon watched Margaret Davis from across the table, still trying to reconcile the woman before him as Ella's mom. He remembered some of her earlier movies and the research he'd done on her and her ex-husband — fallen actor James Berry — and the custody battle Ella had been a part of when she was a child. He remembered all the issues Ella had dealt with because of her mom, how they had shaped the woman he loved.

He took a sip of his water, half-listening to Margaret talking about a new script her agent Richard wanted to send her. He glanced at Ella beside him, recognizing the blankness on her face as her trying to process what she should say instead of what she wanted to say. He squeezed her knee beneath the table and watched a small smile bloom across her face.

"That sounds great, mom. Was Richard happy to see you?" Ella picked a dumpling off one of the small plates they'd ordered while waiting for their main courses, her eyes never leaving her mom.

Margaret laughed, a laugh that rang through the restaurant. Gideon couldn't help but smile at the raspier version of Ella's laugh. They both knew how to light up a room, that was for certain. "Oh, honey, was he! He said I'd never looked better. Dare I say it? He was excited! He said this could be our year." She raised her eyebrows at them, sipping her Shirley Temple. Gideon had seen her stare at the drinks menu when they sat down, the same battle warring in her as it did in him. But she'd opted for the virgin version of one of her favorite drinks. It probably helped that Ella ordered first, and quickly.

Gideon smiled at her. "That's really exciting, Margaret. Will you be in the city more now that you're back to breaking hearts and turning the screen silver?" He kept trying to find things to talk about, but Margaret never left room for a new topic.

"Oh, who knows. One thing at a time." She smiled back at him. "But you guys know all about that, what with Ella being here and you still in that podunk town."

Gideon raised his eyebrows. He hadn't heard that word in ages, and while he loved Sugar Grove, he couldn't disagree. Ella rolled her eyes. Probably not the first time her mom had described the college town that had a way of never changing from its hippie heyday in the 70's.

Their waiter came, setting raw plates of meat on the table around the grill in the center.

"Can I get you guys anything else? Sake, perhaps?" he asked, looking between their faces. Margaret opened her mouth and closed it. She turned her attention to the platter of short ribs.

"No, we're great. Thank you." Ella said, glancing at her mom before throwing the waiter a smile. He nodded and left, clearing their emptied appetizer plates.

Gideon watched the two women, Ella's gaze never leaving her mom, who had suddenly become entirely invested in the food before her. He saw Ella as a young girl, unable to understand her mom's behavior. He saw her as a young woman, realizing she needed to take care of her and her mom if they were going to survive. And he saw Margaret as the woman she once was, young and full of life. Invincible. And how that woman, the one who always wanted the stage, had to live in a separate reality if she was going to continue living outside of Ella's crutch.

"So, Gideon, tell me about yourself. What do you do?" A flash of disappointment disappeared beneath a smile as Margaret looked at him and started cooking some of the meat they'd ordered.

Gideon chewed, realizing Ella really hadn't told Margaret anything about him. He cleared his throat. "Um, well, I'm a musician. The frontman for Eternal Youths. We released our first album in January and we're doing a festival tour this summer." He took a sip of water, watching Margaret freeze.

Her eyes went between him and Ella. "A musician? You didn't say he was a musician." Her mouth was still full. Margaret sat up, finishing her bite, her face bewildered. Ella sighed beside him.

"I didn't think it mattered, mom."

Gideon looked between the two, an interloper in this quiet family feud.

"Didn't matter?" Margaret huffed. "I guess I haven't taught you anything. Well, it's your heart on the line." She pointed her chopsticks at Gideon. "If you fucking hurt her, I will bury you alive so far beneath the ground, no one will ever know you existed. Do you fucking hear me?"

Gideon stared, wide-eyed, at this small woman who inspired as much fear in him as his own mom did. With the drop of a hat, Margaret had gone from fun and loving to ready to put his balls in a vise.

"Um, yeah. Yes, of course." He stumbled over his words. He wanted her to know he'd already learned what it was like to hurt Ella, to lose her, and how that pain would never amount to anything Margaret could do to him. But he knew when to keep his mouth shut.

"Okay, good." Margaret went back to her food, heat still rolling off her. "So. Tour. That's exciting. When do you leave and when do you get back?"

"Mom, maybe we should talk about things other than Gideon's profession," Ella said, her voice tired. "Did I tell you about that new band I've been working with?"

Margaret shot daggers at Ella. "We're not done with that conversation, kid. But for now, fine. The purple weaver-birds one?"

Ella laughed nervously. "They're called Flight of the Purple Birds. Well, you know how they had a show last night? They want me to tour with them in the fall as their on-site publicist. Manage the pre-tour pub and then do the social media and networking during. All expenses paid, plus our usual rate and an on-site bonus."

Gideon watched her explain, loving the excitement in her voice. Ella loved helping people. And she was good at it. Her success with her clients was fast, her results lucrative. He wondered what it was like to have her on tour, her constant warmth and enthusiasm pushing whatever band she was with. While she and Margaret went back and forth, he wondered what it'd be like for Eternal Youths to have her by their side during the summer. He wondered what it'd be like to fully share his band, his work, and every other part of his life with her.

19

The rumble of the passing subway brought Ella out of her daydream, her computer screen coming into focus. In their office, Rachel's tapping on her keyboard was soft, fast while she was hyper-focused with her headphones in. Julie was also engrossed in her work, probably working on the contract for Flight of the Purple Birds. Ella stretched, looking around the bright office space. She had talked to Rachel about the band's offer and, like she figured, Rachel wanted her to take it. And Ella wanted to take it too — she loved traveling and being surrounded by live music, by the creative types who helped a show come to fruition. But being away from Gideon for that long made her heart ache, which would be especially compounded with him being gone for months leading up to that.

Ella glanced over at Rachel. She had proposed Ella take the on-site bonus in its entirety, given the time commitment; she could use some of it to fly Gideon out to visit her, depending on the tour schedule. Rachel had also proposed they take their standard rate the band was paying and put it towards hiring a second publicist for their music clients for while Ella was away. Ella sighed, clicking into her email.

Speaking of the band.

Paul had emailed her, asking if she was available in May to come to a show in New Orleans. Ella put her head in her hands, trying to ignore the headache her schedule was giving her. Gideon left in May. If she was gone before he left, it would be an extra weekend where they wouldn't see each other before the long stretch.

"Hey, Rach?" She looked at her business partner, who was engrossed in her work.

"Hey, Rachel?" Ella said even louder.

Rachel looked over, taking one headphone out. "Sorry, drafting a release for this publishing event. What's up?"

"Paul wants me to go to a show in New Orleans in May. I'm not doing it. I'm sorry, I just... can't."

Rachel's face was blank while she processed

what had been said before she was struck with who Paul was and what the band wanted from Ella.

"Oh! Yeah, no worries. I totally understand, and they'll be taking you from me for months. We'd agreed to the New York City shows this month and for the fall national tour. Anything besides that I'm fine with letting go, feel free to make those calls without me." Rachel smiled and replaced the earbud, turning back to her work.

"Oh, actually — " Rachel took out her bud again. "Could you email our top pick to handle the media clients our offer? The email draft should be in Google Drive, I'd like to get the onboarding started as soon as possible."

"Oh, yeah, absolutely." Ella smiled and Rachel resumed working.

They'd decided on Ruby Delacey, a woman in her late twenties with curly red hair. Her MBA in communications came from Columbia and she was looking to get out of the corporate world — even if it meant taking a pay cut. Ella pulled out her resume, scanning it one last time. She'd interviewed well, especially compared to the younger interviewees, which they'd unfortunately gotten a lot of submissions from thanks to Maven Media's newness to the industry. Everyone wanted a job, but the older ones knew they had a better shot at an established company.

Ella copied and pasted the drafted email from the shared document, reading it one last time before CC'ing Rachel and sending it on its way. If Ruby accepted, they'd have a new person in the office next week. Once Ruby joined, they could sign three media clients and put that money towards hiring a human resources manager. But for the time being, Julie was handling those aspects of the business.

Julie pulled out her headphones and looked at Ella.

"Heya, wanna grab some lunch? I think my stomach's eating itself." She leaned back in her chair, rubbing her flat stomach. Ella smiled. It'd been awhile since they'd spent any alone time together. While Rachel had been folded into their friendship rather seamlessly, Ella and Julie's relationship was still deeper, more sisterly, than Ella's and Rachel's. Ella wanted to tell Julie about Gideon meeting her mom, and how nervous she was about the next few months with the various tour schedules without having to worry about someone putting the business first.

"Sure, as long as you don't mind if I talk your ear off." Ella grinned, going to the door to grab her coat.

"Ha! As long as you don't mind if I talk your ear off." Julie joined her, and they waved to Rachel, who threw them a quick smile but kept her head down.

20

Banging his head against the wall until he bled sounded so much nicer than continuing to listen to Eternal Youths play. More specifically listening to Jack try to play.

Gideon paced around the room while Lucas took a turn explaining to Jack how to play Halo, their first big single from the album released in January. Gideon had gone over it again and again in his head: it wasn't that Jack was bad, per se — he was technically sound — but his playing had a muddled quality. The notes sounded staticky and ran into one another. The original band members had had a separate meeting, opting to not tour with a new single for their second album until Jack could figure out how to play the first album. They all took turns trying to help the guy figure out what he wasn't doing right.

"Okay, let's try this again," Lucas said, his topknot bouncing while he counted off on the drums.

They launched into the song and Gideon closed his eyes, hoping it would limit his exposure to the two trucks backing into each other that was Jack's playing. He was tempted, yet again, to find a guitarist that didn't lead a sober life but knew at this point it was too late to find someone and get them up to speed.

"Please stop."

Tom's voice cut through the noise, pained as he looked at each member. Jack stood in his spot, his baby face furrowed.

"I... I'm sorry, guys. I'm playing it, I just don't know... what else to do."

It was Lucas' turn. "I'm not a guitarist, but can you, I dunno, tighten your strings?"

"Wait." Gideon spun to look at the band. "I'm a total idiot. Jack, when was the last time you took it in for a setup?"

Jack stared blankly at him. "A... what?"

"Dude, a setup. You're supposed to take it in every now and then to get the saddles or truss rod adjusted. You might also need the bridge reset." Gideon had always taken his guitars in once a year or so to get readjusted; he thought every guitarist did that. But Jack was young — all of twenty-three — and had never played in a professional capacity before. No wonder his knowledge was limited.

"Here, try mine." Gideon took his guitar from around his neck, trading Jack for his. They'd already gone over changing the strings, tightening the strings, playing slower, faster, but Gideon had spaced on the more technical aspects of the guitar. Jack's strings were probably too close to the fret board. Jack started playing, and Gideon was filled with hope for the first time in he didn't even know how long. Tom looked like he wanted to cry, shoulders sagging with relief while he watched Jack play.

Jack stopped playing and looked at Gideon.

"Holy shit. I could never figure out why I couldn't sound like this. Thanks, man."

"Of course, but how long have you had that guitar?"

"Since I was fifteen. I just never thought to have it taken in and I don't have the money for a new one."

Gideon looked at Tom. "I could run to my apartment and grab one of my extras. Maybe we'll be able to have regular practice hours since he knows the songs. He'll just have to get a feel for a new guitar."

"Yeah, that sounds good." Tom watched Ryan, Lucas, and Jack going over the songs, now that they could actually hear what Jack was playing. "You know, I'm going to come with you, Gid. I think I left something at your place last I was there." The look on his face had nothing to do with leaving an item at the apartment.

Gideon felt a lump in his throat and tried to swallow it down.

21

Nothing could have prepared Ella for meeting Gideon's mom.

"Darlin', your hair looks great. I promise," he said, giving her hand a squeeze as they climbed the steps to the old building in the West Village. Gideon called the floor and Ella stopped fiddling with her hair, moving on to adjusting her clothes beneath her jacket.

The doors buzzed to let them in, and Ella was surprised at the large marble foyer nestled in the nondescript building. A grand staircase and a green elevator filled the space to her right, a long windowsill on the left doubling as a bench for delivered packages.

"You grew up here?" Her voice echoed through the lobby.

Pain flashed across Gideon's face, vanishing as quickly as it had appeared. "No, my mom moved here when I went to college. Clean slate. For both of us." He stalked over to the elevator, pressing the button. Ella heard it clink down and stop with a thud. He opened the door and they were met with a metal grate Gideon pulled aside with ease, despite it sounding heavy and creaky from the movement.

"We're not... going to die in here, are we?" She raised her eyebrows at him.

He laughed, the warmth of it filling the tight vestibule as he pressed the sixth floor button.

"No, I promise."

The ride was as creaky and harrowing as Ella had imagined, the metal grate just as heavy as she lurched out of the elevator once they reached their destination. The marble hallway was dim, the sconces on the wall emitting a yellow light. Gideon led the way to an apartment at the very end, knocking out a rhythm on the door.

Ella hadn't known what to expect from his mom — she'd never seen pictures — but the woman who stood before her was not it.

Amelia Pike was shorter than Ella, her curly dark hair going every which way. Her frame delicate, her smile wide. Her eyes reminded Ella of looking into Gideon's, only sharper.

"Hi, monkey," Amelia said, giving Gideon a hug and a kiss on the cheek. "You must be Ella." She took Ella into a tight hug. "Please, come in."

She turned into the apartment, heading down a short hallway and disappearing into a room. They followed, Gideon shutting the door behind them while they took off their coats and shoes.

"Monkey, eh?" Ella whispered, trying to hide her laughter.

Gideon rolled his eyes but smiled. "Old habits die hard, okay?"

Ella shook her head, following him to the kitchen. The apartment was warm, light streaming in from all sides, lighting up the off-white paint. The kitchen was open to the living room where one wall sported wallpaper, beautiful lush flowers in shades of pink and red and orange against a dark backdrop. Patterned tapestries hung from the ceiling, meeting around a tin pendant lantern that cast a spotted pattern across the ceiling. Ella stood by the butcher-block island, taking in the patterns and colors, the velvets and furs and woods, throughout the apartment. Vibrant organized chaos.

It was everything Ella wanted for her own place.

She looked at Gideon, understanding him a little more.

"Do you like tea, sweetie?"

Ella was pulled from her reverie. "Oh, yes. I'll take whatever you have, I'm not picky." She smiled at Amelia, her nerves finally subsiding.

"Well, I have enough tea for a Sultan's harem. Besides, it's good for us women to know what we want. It's okay to be a little picky, no?" Amelia raised an eyebrow before rummaging through a cabinet. "You seem like a rose kind of gal. One of these days I'm going to blend my own teas, but until then, I have this rose and eucalyptus. Gideon here likes his Earl Grey and I'm more of a lavender girl myself." She pulled out several boxes and a jar of honey, setting them on the island in front of Ella before opening a different cabinet, taking her time picking mugs.

"Sorry for my mom, she likes to make everything into an event," Gideon said, his voice filled with love while he watched her take mugs out and put them back.

Ella also never would have taken Gideon for a momma's boy.

"Oh, hush you." Amelia kept her back to them, but Ella could hear the smile in her voice.

"I appreciate that, it makes ordinary moments extraordinary." Ella leaned her head against Gideon's arm, watching his mom. She was like a hummingbird, all bright and brilliant but quick and efficient. Gideon put his arm around Ella and kissed the top of her head. Ella wondered if this was what having a real family was like. Where the mom made tea for guests and the children's voices were laced with love when speaking of their relatives. Where black and white photos adorned the walls. Ella bet the holidays were filled with lights and hot chocolate, birthdays with balloons and cake.

A pang shot through her heart. Ella had always known that's what she wanted from life, but it had always been an abstract idea. Being faced with it now, and with the man she loved by her side, she realized just how much she'd missed out on and just how much she wanted those things.

22

Gideon watched his mom curl up on her loveseat, his hand resting on Ella's knee beside him. They took up the couch, Ella's feet tucked under her while she leaned into him. She was laughing about some story his mom was telling about him as a kid, both their laughs filling the small, open space.

"So anyway," his mom said between laughter, "I said, 'Sir, who's Amelia Pike? WHAT HAVE THEY DONE TO YOU?'" They died laughing and Gideon couldn't help but join in. He'd heard the story a million times; when he was little, his family would play Who's Who? They'd invent different names and stories about one another, creating fantasy worlds around them. But they'd do it with no notice, so Gideon learned to be quick on his feet and roll with wherever the wind took them. His mom was almost always the one who started it, usually after his dad addressed her.

Ella's laugh slowly subsided, the smile staying put. "Question. Is your maiden name Pike? I thought Tom's last name was Russo." She glanced at Gideon.

He watched his mom's face fall a little, as it always did when his father came up.

"Yes, Pike is my maiden name. Russo is mine and Gideon's legal name, but I think we both found Pike to be a… more gentle way of living after his father passed." She took a sip of her tea, giving Gideon the look he knew so well.

I love you, I'm sorry, you'll always have me.

"Speaking of family," his mom said, putting her mug down. "Any update on Anthony?"

Gideon hung his head. "Yeah. We're going the rehab route."

When he'd run back to his apartment with Tom during band practice, they'd agreed rehab was the next best step for Anthony. He needed more attention than Tom could give him, between working and managing the house. It didn't help that Anthony had always had an attitude problem; having his dad manage everything from when and what he ate to his medication to his bathroom habits was cause for verbal upheavals.

Gideon looked at Ella and his mom, nodding. They both remained silent, the gravity of the situation settling in.

"Okay, then. I'll call Tom tonight." His mom stood, clearing their empty mugs to kitchen. Gideon looked at Ella again, and she finally met his gaze.

"I'm really sorry, Gideon. Let me know if I can do anything. I'm sure I could help him get into Pinewood. I know it's a bit more expensive, but my mom always did well when she went there."

"Thanks." He rubbed her leg, leaning in to give her a peck on the cheek.

She ran her fingers through his hair, resting them at the base of his neck. Her touch always felt so good, and he allowed himself to sink into it. Gideon's trip with Tom had also consisted of him floating the idea of hiring Maven Media as an outside publicity consultant. 4AD's on-staff publicity team had done the bare minimum. Gideon understood — they were probably overworked and underpaid, most of them in charge of at least twenty acts apiece. They'd only checked off half the items on the proposed marketing list for Eternal Youths. Bringing in an outside firm would help make up the difference. Tom had known Gideon was ultimately getting at bringing Ella along for tour, but they skirted around actually discussing that as the reason. Gideon knew the way to get what he wanted was through facts and numbers, and Tom knew that was the only way to legitimately sell the band — and 4AD — on paying for extra publicity.

23

Ella fell flat onto her bed, Gideon following suit. She laughed at the impact his large frame made. They'd stayed at Amelia's until after they'd finished ordered-in pizza, laughing and hanging out. Ella knew how Gideon had gotten his hard exterior, but being surround by the warmth of his mom had showed her where all his hidden softness came from.

She raised herself on one elbow, head in her hand. Gideon's face was relaxed while he stared back, his hair falling in his eyes. She pushed it aside and ran her fingers through his hair, taking her time with the mini-massage. Gideon closed his eyes and moaned. Adjusting, he rested his head on his arms, stretching his body out. Ella moved her hand down his neck, trailing the ridge of his muscular shoulders. She traced the length of his spine, goosebumps running along his back as she moved. Ella loved looking at him, touching him. Moments like these, she could see their future. Their aches and blessings, their support and fear. She could see the way they'd hold each other, love each other, their glass hearts becoming a single diamond.

Her fingers found their way to his arms, to the tattoos that wound their way around his muscles. Vines and flowers, Shiva and Hanuman and Vishnu. Centers, reminders. She leaned forward, kissing his bicep where a marigold sat. The kiss turned to laughter when he flexed beneath her lips.

"You're ridiculous." She swatted him as he laughed and rolled onto his back, clutching his stomach.

"I had to, I'm sorry."

Ella sat up, shaking her head. She licked her lips, watching his abs flex with his subsiding laughter, falling in love all over again with his hot goofiness.

"Your mom's really amazing, Gideon." She pushed her hair behind her ears, hit with the unfamiliar pang of what it meant to have a family that loved you wholly. Ella knew her mom loved her, but it was so often hidden beneath Margaret's love for herself. Amelia had shown her a different kind of family.

Gideon sat up and pulled Ella between his legs, looping her legs over his so their noses were touching. His hands held her face, gingerly.

"I'm lucky, I know that. But she also taught me what an amazing *woman* was. And I'm even more lucky to have you in my life. If we ever have a family, I have no doubt that's the kind of mom you would be."

His words froze Ella. They had never talked about having a family. They'd only ever touched on marriage once, in the abstract "one day" kind of way. But seeing all they'd gone through, a part of Ella had always known they'd ultimately get married to one another. She tried to picture what it would be like to have a family with Gideon, and was even more surprised at how easy it was, how right it felt.

Ella's shoulders relaxed, and she kissed him. Deeply, breathing him in. Not knowing when they'd be able to see each other after this visit. She pulled away. How could they move forward if there was no end in sight for their current situation?

"What's wrong, darlin'?" Gideon asked.

Damn her and her inability to hide anything she was thinking.

"Just... this situation." She bit her lower lip. She didn't want to talk about it — the last time they had, it'd turned into an argument — but the shakiness of their future was becoming too much to bear.

Gideon nodded, lowering his gaze. "It's finite, Ella. I might have my weekends back. There was something wrong with Jack's guitar so we switched it and it's a million times better. We just have to get through the summer tour."

Confusion hit Ella like a ton of bricks. Did he really forget about her being on tour immediately after he was done with his?

"Um, babe?" She tilted her head. "I'm going on tour with Flight of the Purple Birds September to November. So, let's just say you don't get your weekends back, we need to figure out how we're going to see each other from April until November."

The look on his face confirmed her thoughts.

"Oh… Right. Well, we will work it out, Ella. One day at a time. In September I'll move here and the guys will follow, and then when you're back we can start fresh."

"Okay, but I'm asking you to help me figure out what to do in the meantime." Ella tried to tamp down the fire that was building inside her. She'd known Gideon could illicit the strongest passion she'd ever felt — she just hadn't expected that to include disagreements.

Gideon's own posture straightened, his face hardening.

"And I'm saying we'll have to figure it out as we come to it because I just don't know."

"And I'm saying that doesn't work for me." Ella felt the heat in her cheeks. They'd had their fair share of problems in the past, but she really hadn't thought trying to figure out how to make their schedules work was going to be one of them going forward.

And she really hadn't expected to get an attitude in response.

24

Was she for real?

Gideon tried to focus on his breathing, to pull calming energy from his chakras. But her stiff jaw and rosy cheeks made him want to say fuck it.

Ella was pissed, and god help him, it was turning him on.

They stared off, the tension between them palpable, Gideon trying not to focus on her being between his legs and Ella probably trying not to escalate the discussion into an argument.

Gideon took a deep breath. "Okay. Okay. I..." Was now a good time to mention asking Tom about hiring Maven Media for the festival tour? He had no idea. And he was torn between seeing how angry they could get and channeling that into hot make-up sex, or taking more deep breaths and talking about their options.

"You what?"

Oh, Darlin' wanted to fight. He had to stop himself from grinning. They'd never had a real fight before. The last argument hadn't felt good, but they had been short on time and it felt sprung on him. But now? Ella had always made him feel alive. They could get into it really quick and then take their time making up. He'd take his time making sure she knew how much he wanted her.

"Again, I don't know what to tell you. We both want me down here in the city, but I can't do that before tour. Not with band practices happening so frequently. I can't deal with breaking my lease and finding a new spot in six weeks. So tell me, sweetheart, what you think our options are."

He knew using a pet name in an argument sounded condescending. But he couldn't stop it from slipping out. At the name, Ella's eyes went wide and a small smile played at her lips. Yeah, that was a line he might've crossed.

"Well, *babe*, I figured we could at least *talk* about our options. If you can't move here before tour, and I'm gone after tour, we should probably discuss traveling options. I don't know what you guys can and can't do on this tour of yours." Her voice was measured, but the heat was apparent.

"Ella, we're going to be *on tour*. You know what that means — in and out of venues, on the road, schmoozing with people. I'm not exactly going to have a lot of free time to spend with you."

"Are you for real right now, Gideon? Do you honestly think I care HOW we spend our time together? God forbid I just want to SEE you." Her rising voice was followed by a cold front when she removed herself from between his legs. She stood, staring at him, her breathing heavy. "But fine, I DO know what that means. So me visiting you for a day here and there is off the table. Now we can discuss other options."

Gideon stood directly before her, their bodies almost touching. Her face was tilted up, hands on her hips. He was reminded of a similar position last year, when he'd shown up at her office after radio silence for over a year. She'd kicked him out, but that hadn't stopped him from getting so close she'd gasped.

He leaned down, his lips next to her ear.

"How would you feel about mixing business with pleasure?" His tongue tickled her earlobe, pulling it into his mouth. He lightly bit and pulled, her body melting against his, before letting go and pulling back. He looked down at Ella, her anger turning into a different kind of fire. She swayed a little, looking up at him.

"What do you mean?"

Gideon smiled, loving the way she reacted to him. "I didn't want to say anything yet because it's still up in the air, but I asked Tom if there was a way we could use Maven Media and have you come on tour with us."

Ella stared at him before a smile started to break. "Wait... Really? Rachel told me I should talk to you about doing that."

"Damn, why didn't you say anything?" He couldn't believe his ears.

"Why didn't YOU?"

Gideon laughed. "I just did! And everything is still up in the air so I didn't want to get your hopes up."

"Well, we would've needed to talk about whether or not we want to work together," Ella said, snorting and throwing her hands up.

Gideon rolled his eyes. "Well, gee, I'm sorry I didn't think to ask if you wanted to work together before I floated the idea to Tom about hiring you and your company to help us out so you and I could spend more time together. So I guess I'm asking you now."

"Asking me what?"

Goddamn, she was infuriating. "Do you want to work together, Ella?"

"If it means seeing you, yes. Of course I want to work with you."

They faced off, voices loud, panting.

"Okay. Good. I want that, too."

"Okay. Good."

The tension hadn't released with their admissions. Gideon sighed, wanting to direct some of the tension to more productive endeavors.

"I'm sorry I got heated."

Ella looked away. "Me, too."

"Hey." Gideon cocked his head, his hand going to the back of her neck. "You know what I think?" She looked at him.

"I think you've been bad."

She raised her face to his, a smile spreading.

"Oh, yeah? What are you going to do about it?"

25

Ella had heard of hot make-up sex, but she'd never had the chance to experience it.

Until now.

There was nothing gentle about the way Gideon kissed her, pushed her to the edge of the bed. Nothing gentle about the way he flipped her around, pushing her torso down. Ella groaned, losing herself to the press of his erection against her ass, his hands kneading each cheek. Every cell in her body craved him and the intense pleasure he supplied. With Gideon, the ache between her thighs was insatiable.

"Spread your legs."

Especially when he talked to her like that.

She obliged, feeling one hand slip between her folds.

"Oh, baby. You're so wet."

His moan made her whimper, wanting so much more.

Slap!

Her back arched with the sting from his spank, cooled off by a kiss he planted on her cheek, his hand massaging the place he'd hit. Ella arched her back more, pressing her hips back into him, his massive bulge straining against his pants.

"Gideon," she panted. A liquid heat coursed through her body, making the emptiness inside her unbearable.

The sting from a second slap caused her to cry out, to buck with pleasure as the wave of desire washed over her.

"Ask nicely, darlin'."

She heard him unbutton, unzip his pants, the whisper of fabric falling to the ground. She felt his thick head push against her entrance, his arm wrap around her waist, finding her clit. He grazed it with his fingers, pushing a little with his hips, teasing her body with the power he possessed. He knew he made her breathless, weak in the knees. He knew it was so much fun to be reminded.

"Please, Gideon. I need you."

"That's my girl." He pushed inside her, teasing her clit as he slid between her slick folds. Ella's body trembled beneath him. He sat inside her dripping heat, hard as stone, the pressure in her core mounting to a tsunami. Gideon kept his hands on her hips, holding her as tight against him as possible before dragging each inch of his cock from her pussy. Her body missed him immediately, desperate for him to fill her again.

She got her wish as he pushed harder, finding a rhythm where her ass slapped against his hips, his muscled thighs, his grunts in time with her pants. Her hands clutched the sheets before her, twisting them as the pressure in her core built, the release she'd longed for within reach. His fingers dug into her pelvis, her skin, marking her. He always made sure she knew she was his. But he also made sure she knew he was hers, too.

"No, faster," Ella panted as his thrusts slowed.

"I want to watch you come, darlin'."

He peeled his body from hers, their skin covered in a thin sheen of sweat. Ella propped herself on her arms, her body shaking from the prolonged bend over the bed and the force with which Gideon had pounded into her. He gave her ass a light squeeze and she flopped onto her back, her breathing heavy.

But this view was so much better.

Gideon stood before her, all man and all muscle.

A god. His defined torso glinted in the dim light, the tattoos on his chiseled arm rippling as his stroked his massive length. His eyes were glazed with desire, watching her. A flood of desire rolled through her. Ella reached for him, desperate to touch him. To pull him against her until she didn't know where she ended and he began.

26

As if stroking himself wasn't making him hard enough, having Ella on her back — her goddess body exposed — was certainly doing the trick.

She reached for him, her divine chest heaving. His cock was heavy, full, in his hand, slick with their mingled essences. He settled between her legs, leaning over until his mouth closed over hers. Their tongues sparred, desperate to become one with the other. Ella tangled her fingers in his hair, pushing herself against him, drawing him closer. Gideon cupped her neck, his thumb tracing her jaw, inhaling her warm scent.

Vanilla and sandalwood.

Home.

When he finally pulled away, he met Ella's eyes,

laced with desire. With need. Gideon cupped her breasts, his fingers teasing the nipples to hardened peaks. He kissed her neck, tugging her earlobe into his mouth, sucking while she moaned. He moved to her neck, grazing the sensitive skin with his tongue, his teeth, biting and licking until she cried out. She was on the edge, ready to break.

So was he.

He trailed his kisses to her chest, giving each rosebud equal attention with his mouth. Pulling and sucking, swirling and moaning against her skin, sliding his cock into the petals of her sex. The heat she offered enveloped him and he grunted at the shock from being out in the cold, away from her, for so long. He hovered his body over hers, taking his time moving in and out of her heavenly body, watching the expression on her face change. Watching her eyes close, her chest heave against his, her skin flushed. Hearing her gasps, the sound of his name on her lips.

He pushed and pulled, her hips meeting his with each plunge, each need to send her over the edge. He sped up, holding her as close to him as his pace allowed. He wanted her pleasure to break her into a million pieces, needed her body to clench around his as he gave her every piece of him, body and soul. Her cries mingled with his as they came, their bodies overtaken by an earthquake that shattered them. Ella mindlessly grasped at him, her lips searching until they met his.

Gideon collapsed on top of her, his tongue invading her mouth as he moaned against her, deepening their kiss. She held his face between her hands, softly biting and tugging his lower lip before releasing him from her grasp. But Gideon knew she'd never release him from her heart. He stared into her eyes, their noses touching as he breathed her in, still unable to believe his luck at having this woman in his arms. In his bed. In his soul. He would never have the words to tell her how much he loved her. He slid beside her, folding her against him, her slender arms wrapping around his torso. Her fingers lightly traced his back, sending goosebumps erupting across his skin. He felt his cock twitch at the sensation, the thought of another round.

But until then, Gideon wanted to hold onto her, to feel her heated skin against his, to smell the vanilla of her shampoo as her head nestled beneath his chin. He wanted to hold on to her forever. To have nights like this one, to have whatever the next morning brought.

His heart ached with the need to begin the rest of their lives and the realization that one lifetime would never be enough.

27

Her body still tingled from her weekend with Gideon. Ella could only imagine how being surrounded by him, living with him, would feel. She'd be floating every damn day.

Pollack followed her down the hall to the kitchen. The apartment was quiet, a note on the island letting her know Rachel was off visiting a client with Julie. They'd discussed getting any out-of-office work done before Ruby started on Wednesday. While they were out, Ella was going to take advantage of working from home while she could. Ella grabbed her coffee mug and filled it, taking it to the living room. She was still thinking about Amelia, the window into the life she was wanting more and more. Conversations with Amelia had been filled with love and compassion, curiosity and non-judgement. Amelia asked about everyone she knew in Gideon's life, they talked about books and podcasts, she'd asked Ella all sorts of questions. They'd curled up on couches in a brightly lit room splashed with colors, eucalyptus and bergamot and lavender wafting through the air. When Ella and Gideon had gone to lunch with her mom, the conversations were almost entirely steered towards Margaret. The glory days, the people, lost projects, upcoming projects. It was endless. She'd asked few questions about Ella and even fewer about Gideon — especially after finding out he was a musician.

But she'd asked, which was something Margaret didn't use to do unless she wanted to pick a fight. Ella sighed. She should call her mom.

It took a few rings for Margaret to answer, but when she did, it was mid-laugh.

"Hey, kid. How's it going?" Her voice held the remnants of a chuckle, her gravelly voice light.

"It's... good. How are you?" Ella tried to mask her surprise. She couldn't remember the last time her mom had been up this early, let alone laughing about something. Or being with someone.

An immediate wave of anxiety washed over her when Margaret said something to someone, her voice muffled. Ella was used to her mom parading men around, but it was usually a thing she did drunk.

"Glad to hear it. How's that boy of yours, the musician?"

"Gideon?" Ella rolled her eyes. "He's good. What are you up to?"

Her mom laughed at something someone said. "I'm hanging out with my friend Jaxton. We haven't seen each other in years."

Ella froze. "Jaxton... Jax? Didn't you date him when I was twelve?"

"Yes! I'm surprised you remember him, it was only a couple months."

Ella heard her mom open and close a door, the muffled silence of being alone following her. "In any case, back then we were both nightmares. He's been sober ten years, we got back in touch, and now here we are."

Ella picked at her nails. At least he was truly sober, whereas her mom was just now inching up on sobriety six months post-rehab. She didn't remember Jax well, just blurry images of him and Margaret dancing in the kitchen or falling onto the couch. And the floor.

"Well... That's good. I'm glad you're having fun."

"It's been a breath of fresh air, lemme tell you.

Like seeing you last weekend, that was nice. Wasn't it?"

Ella could hear the hint of validation in her voice.

"Yeah, mom, it was. Gideon liked you," Ella said. "Did... Did you like him?"

Speaking of wanting validation.

Her mom was quiet for a moment. "You know? I actually did. I didn't want to. But it's plain as the nose on your face how much he loves you. And he seems to have his head on straight. Has he figured out what to do about moving and touring?"

Those were the last words Ella had expected her mom to say, especially asking about tour. That had been a passing point in their conversation, one sentence and they'd moved onto one of Margaret's stories about going to visit one of her musician friends on tour back in the 90's. But she'd remembered, which gave Ella a flickering of hope that maybe — just maybe — this past time in rehab was her last.

"Um, wow, okay. Yeah, he's the best." Ella said. "I'm lucky."

Her mom made a noise. "Well, so is he. And don't you forget it. But tell me about the tour situation."

Ella took a deep breath before launching into their plan of getting Tom and 4AD to hire Maven Media for the festival season and Gideon's plan to move to the city in September. How they were planning on moving in together either then or the following year, but weren't sure how fast they wanted to take that jump. Or if they even needed to yet, knowing they were going to stay together.

"Hm. You're sure it's a good idea to work with your lover? And, kid, from experience, I can tell you that you absolutely should live with someone before planning on spending your life with them." Ella heard the hiss of a lighter, the drag of a breath.

Of course her mom would switch addictions, replacing alcohol with her forgotten habit of smoking. But Ella would take that over relapse any day.

Ella sighed. Her mom had always rushed into living with guys, or having guys live with them, and it hadn't turned out so well. Ella felt confident she and Gideon would be fine — they were best friends, they were lovers. They were both clean and had shared interests. They wanted the same things, the same life. She knew there was no right way to do this, but this was the way she wanted it done. Ella bit her tongue, not wanting to lob her mother's past in her face.

"I understand where you're coming from, mom. But I'm going to make my own decisions and I'll live with the consequences."

"Okay. Just don't say I didn't warn you." Her mom exhaled. "Hey, I gotta go, but it was nice hearing from you, kid. Love you."

"Love you, too, mom." They hung up, and Ella released the breath she'd been holding. That went nowhere near as bad as she'd thought it would, and the hope she'd felt grew.

28

The coffee was as weak as Gideon remembered, but at least it helped wash down the cookies Joe always brought to the AA meetings. The other members sometimes brought other treats, and Gideon knew it would be a good night if chocolate doughnuts were on the table after the meeting wrapped.

They weren't.

Gideon took another bite of the chocolate chip cookie in his hand, half listening to Amy and a couple other members standing in a circle by the refreshments table. They were close enough to the cookies that Gideon could probably just reach over and…

Amy touched his arm. "Aren't you and Ella doing long distance?"

Damnit. So close.

"Um, yeah. Why?" Gideon had no idea where in the conversation they were. He took a bite of his cookie.

"Oh, well we were just talking about the strain of long distance." Amy looked at him. "I figured you'd be able to give some input since it's poor Olivia's first time with it sober."

Gideon nodded, looking at the faces around him to determine which one was Olivia. The tall one directly across from him playing with her hair seemed to be a good bet.

"Yeah, it's not easy. Honestly, keeping busy is the best way to manage. Going to extra meetings, too." Ella flashed through his mind, their last encounter heating him to his core. He could hardly wait for the day when they lived together, when every day he could wrap himself around her.

The group took the conversation into ways to keep busy, and Gideon took his opportunity to busy himself with getting more cookies. He excused himself from the group and stood in front of the various platters.

"Hey, Pike," Amy said, coming up by his elbow. Her hair was loose this time, the curls brushing his arm. She pushed her glasses up her nose, turning to him.

"Hey, Ames." Gideon grabbed a couple extra cookies and some sort of tan brownie. He knew he liked them but could never remember their name.

"So... how's it going? We haven't caught up in a bit. Are you managing the long distance okay?"

Gideon turned to her. "Yeah, so far so good. It'll be a tough couple of months, but I'm actually working with Tom on hiring her to go on tour with us this summer before she heads on tour with a band for the fall."

"Oh, that'd be good." Amy hid her surprise with a smile. "And then I guess you'll be leaving us for good, when you move down to the city?"

"Yeah, just a little. Currently looking for an engagement ring to make it a bit more official but the search has been a dead end."

"Oh, wow... That's a big step. I didn't know you guys were so serious. Or had spent that much time with each other." Amy had always warned Gideon of going too fast, of taking his time. Especially when it came to Ella. "What about Anthony? How's he doing?"

Her subject change was accompanied with her turning to the table, eying the treats.

"He's... okay. Tom and I are going to talk to him about rehab, we think he's been abusing his Oxy."

He took a bite of his cookie, tempted to get more of the coffee to wash the preservatives down.

Amy whipped around. "Your alcoholic cousin is on Oxy after a drunk car crash and isn't in rehab? That's a bold move, Pike. I'm... surprised. He needs help."

Gideon looked at her, unsure of the hostility he felt rolling off her. Amy had always been the sweetest person in the room, always offering a smile and a hug. She took her time to really listen, to understand and respond with compassion.

"Yeah, that's why we're going to approach him about rehab"

"Okay, but hasn't it been what, five, six months since the accident?"

Gideon took a step back. "Seriously, Amy? We did what we thought was best. I don't need your judgement on top of everything else."

He threw out his coffee cup, taking the treats to grab his jacket from his chair. He really could not believe what he had heard. That was some bullshit. After everything he'd told her, all the times she'd brought him back from the edge, and she was going to judge him about his family? And his relationship?

Yeah, fuck that.

Pushing through the church doors to the cold,

Gideon practically stomped down the street. The fifteen minute walk to his apartment would help clear his head. He had enough on his plate without having to deal with Amy's attitude over things that didn't concern her.

29

"Okay, but what if we moved our Girl's Night to, I dunno, a weeknight? So that way we don't have to worry too much about various events. Or dates," Rachel said, taking a healthy drink of wine while Julie stretched out on the sectional, her feet landing in Ella's lap. Ella threw her arms over her friend's legs and bit her bottom lip, weighing the options. Their schedules had finally aligned and they were able to have their overdue Girl's Night. With Ella working at least one weekend night, plus balancing her schedule with Gideon's, and Julie still settling in to her life in New York City, and Rachel always going out or spending time with family, they rarely saw each other. Girl's Night had always been every other weekend, but maybe it was time to switch things up.

"Actually, that's not a bad idea. I feel like

Mondays we're always home." Julie's feet wriggled as she said it, a smile forming.

"Oooo! Monday's are also Bach Night!" From her spot on the floor, Rachel spun to look at Ella and Julie. "Since I don't want to start getting into reality TV, we could have our own version and live tweet updates of our movies, like their fan base does. That would get Maven Media's name out there while fitting our brand, plus we'd be having fun."

Ella smiled. Rachel was always their Idea Girl. "Rachel, that's brilliant."

"Actually, Rach." Julie sat up, refilling her wine glass from the box on the modern glass coffee table. "We could do it every week instead and make it kind of like a show for people to tune into. Maybe eventually we could update it to video?"

"Yes!" Rachel jumped up, heading to the kitchen for more pizza.

"Actually, maybe not video. Girl's Night lets us talk about all sorts of things, ya know?" Ella said. She didn't exactly want the world to know her boy problems. Or her problems with her mom. Her phone vibrated against her leg, Gideon's name popping up on the screen.

Hey, what're you up to?

He was never so short when he texted. She

responded, Julie joining Rachel in the kitchen while they talked about the new Girl's Night details.

He texted back immediately. *Can I call you?*

Ella stared at her screen. She hated to interrupt the time with her friends for a guy, especially since they rarely saw each other anymore. But she also could tell when something was wrong with him, and Gideon wasn't just any guy. She stood, grabbing a slice of pizza while she listened to her friends.

"Hey, guys." Ella took a bite of the lukewarm piece. "I'm really sorry, but I need to call Gideon real quick. Something's off."

The girls stopped their chatter, glancing at one another before staring at Ella.

"Yeah, sure. Totally understand," Rachel said, nodding.

"Yeah, totally." Julie gave a forced smile before taking her plate back to the couch.

"Good luck." Rachel followed Julie, their voices resuming, though with less excitement than before.

Ella looked at them before heading to her room, the phone ringing. She felt like she couldn't make anyone happy.

"Hey, handsome." She closed the door behind her, taking a seat on her bed. "I can't talk for too long, but what's up?"

"Amy was being weird at the meeting tonight. I dunno, I... I just needed to hear your voice." His sigh traveled through the phone and Ella felt it in her aching heart.

"Weird how?"

She heard a plastic container opening, the scrape of a utensil on a plate. She smiled, picturing his arms flexing as he dished himself some food.

"Weird like... judgmental? A group of us were talking after and we started talking about long-distance relationships while sober. I mentioned how we were doing fine and she seemed really surprised. And then she asked about Anthony."

Ella laid back, settling against her pillows. Only one reason could account for his sponsor being weird about him being in a serious relationship, especially if she hadn't known he was in one. Ella didn't like the sound of what he said, but she also knew Gideon didn't return any feelings Amy *might* have towards him. Tackling one new issue at a time seemed to be the best bet right now since they were already struggling with the distance. Amy was another problem for another day. "What did she say about Anthony?"

"I mentioned how we were going to talk to him about rehab and she wasn't happy about him not being there already. She made it sound like we'd done wrong by him by not immediately having that as an option after the accident."

She heard him take a bite. "Because of him having an addictive personality and needing to be on meds?" she asked.

"Basically."

"I'm sorry, Gideon. Maybe she was just worried and it came out wrong? She probably has some experience with that kind of thing, but you were trying to do what you thought was best. I'm sure she'll calm down."

It was quiet for a moment before his soft, "Yeah," came through.

"Gideon, it'll be okay. She probably has some of her own shit going on. What are you up to tonight?" Ella bit her lip, hoping the subject change would help take his mind off Amy. Ella hated to think he was worried about his sponsor's reaction to how he was handling his cousin, but she especially hated to think Amy's reaction to them dating was because of hidden feelings Gideon couldn't pick up on.

"Got me some Mexican food, probably just going to watch a movie or something. What about you?"

"Girl's Night, we have pizza and we're watching a

bad horror movie. We also have a cool idea for our business going forward, so that's exciting."

"Oh, awesome. Can't wait to hear about it later, I know you have to go." The silence stretched, neither one of them wanting to be the first to hang up. Every time they did, Ella felt a piece of her heart disappear.

"I wish you were here, darlin'." He let out a long breath, and she closed her eyes to move through the pain in her chest.

"Me too, honey. It was nice to hear your voice."

"Same. Thanks for calling, have a good rest of your night." A kissing sound came through the phone, and she smiled, sending one back. They hung up, and Ella took a few breaths before rejoining her friends.

30

"He's been in his room all day."

Tom stared at Gideon, hands in his lap. Defeat in his voice. Gideon leaned back against the black leather couch in his uncle's living room, trying to figure out how they were going o approach Anthony about getting help.

"Okay. And his meds are in there?"

Tom sighed. "Yeah. He won't let me in, but he also hasn't eaten in at least a day. He just yells at me. I think he knows things are coming to a head."

"Again." Gideon added, thinking back to his conversation with Anthony last year, days before the accident. Anthony had broken down, and they'd agreed rehab was the next step. After the accident, when Anthony moved back in with Tom, they'd thought that was enough to kick Anthony into sobriety. Gideon hadn't expected to be in this position again. Or to have it be about pills instead of alcohol. They'd done their fair share of drugs in college and the following years, when the band was first forming. But when the drugs had started getting in the way, Tom had asked Gideon to cut them out a couple years ago. Gideon had found it surprisingly easy; getting high wasn't his thing. But a couple fingers of whiskey definitely was.

He'd thought Anthony would be the same.

They sat in silence, waiting. For what, Gideon didn't know. Someone would have to do something. He could see the worry etched on Tom's face and knew it'd have to be him. He'd have to find the will to walk back to Anthony's room, to confront whatever lay beyond the door.

"Okay." Gideon nodded, knowing the sooner he did it, the sooner it'd be over. Tom watched him stand, giving him a sad smile. A thank you.

Gideon made his way down the hall to Anthony's room at the end. It felt longer than usual.

Haunted.

He rapped the rhythm he used when visiting his mom, drawing strength from the comforting sound. When Anthony didn't respond, Gideon rapped again, louder.

"What?" The sheer hostility in Anthony's voice made Gideon take a deep breath and breathe it out slowly. He went to go in but found the knob locked.

"Hey, man. It's me."

"What do you want?"

Gideon ran through the different answers and what they could possibly elicit. The only one that might work was the truth. "I don't know, Ant. Can I come in?"

Silence was followed by the thumping of Anthony's crutches, the door unlocking. The thumping moved away from the door, and Gideon let himself in.

The shades were drawn, the room musty and holding the smell of mild B.O. Anthony sat at the edge of his bed, his casted leg in front of him beside his crutches. His shirtless frame was thin, ghostly. He slowly raised his face to meet Gideon's, his black hair greasy, blue eyes dim. Gideon made his way to the bed, haltingly, not wanting to frighten Anthony. He crouched before his cousin.

"Hey, man." Gideon felt like he was talking to a child, and a vivid memory of being six and Anthony having the flu for a week crossed his mind. Gideon wanted to be gentle, but he also knew when push came to shove, they needed

Anthony to see he was the only one who could save himself.

Anthony stared at his lap.

"I... I think you know why I'm here, Ant."

"Yeah." It came as a barely audible whisper, and Gideon released the breath he'd been holding. Anthony met his eyes, and Gideon could see the pupil dilation even in the dim light.

"How many did you take, man?" Gideon glanced around, not finding the pill bottle anywhere.

"Just a couple." Anthony's voice was soft, mirroring the defeat Gideon had seen in Tom's face. Gideon nodded, moving to sit beside his cousin.

"Okay, was that the last of them?"

"Yeah."

"Why wouldn't you let Tom in?" Gideon kept his voice soft, his hand moving to Anthony's back. He could feel the knobs of his cousin's spine and stopped himself from recoiling at his deterioration.

Anthony turned his head to look at Gideon. "I couldn't. His eyes."

"What do you mean, Ant?"

"His eyes. Windows to the sad, sad soul." Anthony looked back at his hands.

Gideon watched his cousin sit there. He'd felt threatened by himself and the pain he'd caused around him, a feeling Gideon knew well. But he was high enough to not put up a fight, and Gideon was going to take this opportunity.

"Yeah, we're all sad, Anthony. Aren't you?" Gideon rubbed his hand along Anthony's back.

Anthony took a deep breath and let it out, a whimper escaping. He dropped his head in his hands while his body was wracked with sobs.

"Hey, man. It's okay. We're here for you." Gideon watched him cry. "Always."

"I need help." His words came as gasps between sobs. A noise came from the door and Gideon looked up, seeing Tom. Tears streamed down his face as he knelt before his son.

"And that's okay, Anthony. We all need help sometimes. I love you — we love you — and we're going to get you help. Does that sound good?"

Gideon watched his family, Anthony hiccuping out a "yes" while Tom crouched to pull his son into his arms. It was moments like these when Gideon was hit with the wave of sadness that he didn't have his dad, and he never would. He stood, giving Tom a small smile over the top of Anthony's head. They didn't need words for Tom to understand Gideon would give them their space, that Gideon would be there when it was time.

He left Tom holding his son against his chest, the wails flowing through the spacious house as he closed the door behind him. He knew this was it, that Anthony would get the help he needed and they could move forward. All of them.

31

Ella turned to face their new employee, who was smiling just as big as she was. Ruby was starting at Maven Media, and her energy was already a welcome light to the office. The sun streaming through the large windows lit her curly hair on fire, the red and gold intertwining as she looked around the open space.

"Wow, I'm so excited," Ruby said, following Ella to her desk. Rachel and Ella had situated it beside Julie's against the wall across from the kitchenette, so their desks combined to make an L-shape. It helped keep the office open and airy, and they could easily talk to one another without raising their voices.

"Okay, so I'll help get you set up with our

company email. You'll be handling our TV and media clients which right now are BRICK Talent, B23 Productions, and World Talent. Rachel manages our publishing clients and I handle music. Julie does the legal work and currently some HR stuff, but we're working on hiring a rep." Ella took a deep breath and smiled. Saying everything out loud helped reinforce their success and just how far they'd come in the last two years since starting the company. Ella remembered working two part-time jobs to support herself while she started her own company before meeting Rachel, whose dad had helped finance the start of Maven Media.

"Amazing, thank you." Ruby took a seat and booted up her computer while Ella went back to her desk.

Ella glanced at Julie as she passed her, but her attention was trained on her computer. Ever since Girl's Night, Julie had been more aloof to Ella. But she couldn't figure out why. Rachel played the cool as a cucumber third party, treating everyone the same even though Ella had a feeling she and Julie talked.

Ella sighed, sending Ruby the onboarding information for their various office platforms. She hated when something was off, but she hated even more when no one talked about it. She thought of Ben, her old friend still up in Sugar Grove. He was always so great about being honest. She missed his company but knew after this last semester of grad school, he'd take his English degree and find a job in New York City at a publishing house.

Looking around, she realized she might not be as close to the people in her life as she'd originally thought. She knew she needed to be better about focusing on her girl friends during the limited time they had together outside of work. The passive aggressiveness that sometimes plagued her female friendships didn't help, but she also noticed that everyone in the office worked with their headphones in. While it helped them all focus, the office felt a little dead to Ella. She wondered if she could get everyone on board with putting in a speaker and starting a Maven Media playlist, where everyone could add songs they were listening to at that time.

"Hey, El?" Rachel's voice cut through her thoughts.

"What's up?" Ella looked at her friend.

Rachel popped a headphone out. "Has Flight of the Purple Birds signed the fall tour contract? I'm trying to update our Google Calendar but don't want to put anything that isn't signed off on or doesn't have first payment."

Ella pursed her lips, trying to remember if she had gotten the signed contracts back. She couldn't, so she turned to her email, searching for them.

"Hey, um, Ella?" Ruby's voice called out.

"Give me oooone minute, Ruby," Ella said, trying not to sigh as her phone buzzed on the desk.

She turned back to Rachel. "I'm not seeing anything, I'll email them now. That's odd, I thought we'd gotten them." She thought about it, realizing Julie might have missed the email since she was getting settled into the company. "Hey, Julie? Jules?"

Her friend looked up, also taking an earphone out. "Sorry, what?"

"Did we get those contracts for Flight of the purple Birds out yet?"

"Oh, shit." Julie laid her head on the desk. "No, goddamnit. I'll do those today."

"Hey, Ella?" Ruby asked.

Ella had a headache and it was barely noon. She couldn't wait until they had enough staff so that everyone wasn't stretched so thin. She couldn't wait until her main focus was touring with bands or — better yet — managing the employees who toured for Maven Media. Then she could go home to Gideon every night, or go on tour with him. She smiled at Ruby and stood. She couldn't have dreamt how far the business had come in the past two years.

Which boded well for the next two years.

32

Gideon shut the door behind him and looked around at the soaring trees, the white mansion tucked among them. It'd been awhile since he'd been completely surrounded by trees, the smell of pine and the sound of chirping birds, and he immediately felt a sense of peace. This would be a good place for Anthony to be. He shoved his hands in his pockets and looked at his uncle and brother, who stood staring at the facility. Waiting for the last moment before saying goodbye.

The large white portico with the burgundy door of Pinewood Rehabilitation reminded Gideon of another era, when the countryside of New York was still being settled. Situated in the mountains outside Sugar Grove, Pinewood was the same place Ella's mom Margaret had gone — several times. But the times she was sober longest had always come after this program. It was expensive, highly sought after, and Ella had asked her mom to call them about getting Anthony a spot. They were able to skip the initial interview but paid a little extra for the immediate care with money Tom had taken from savings and Gideon had taken from his engagement ring budget. But Gideon would have gladly paid it tenfold to get Anthony the best care he could find.

Anthony took a deep breath, and Gideon looked over at his cousin hunched over his crutches. Anthony used to make anyone swoon; his smile was reminiscent of Tom Cruise, his eyes a deep blue. He'd had charm that was unmatched, a presence that took up whole rooms. But the man Gideon saw before him was a shadow of who Gideon once knew. His shoulders sagged, his frame tall but now lanky. His skin, sallow. And Gideon couldn't remember the last time he'd seen him smile.

"Alrighty then." Tom broke the silence. He looked stronger than Gideon had seen him in weeks. The situation with Anthony had worn him down, but now that there was a definite course of action, Tom could stop feeling helpless. Gideon knew he hated to be idle, that he needed some sort of plan. When his brother, Gideon's father, had passed, he'd come over almost every day to make sure Gideon and his mom were taken care, that the house was cleaned and food was served. Gideon thought about what Tom would do once Anthony was out of the house, but kept coming up empty.

"Alrighty then," Anthony said, taking a couple steps on the gravel drive, beginning their exodus from their old life.

The door creaked when it opened, a heavy oak of faded grandeur. But the lobby was modern and bright. Lavender and eucalyptus hit Gideon's nose, the receptionist smiling from behind a dark wood desk, the high polish reflecting the gold lights around them. They drifted forward, unsure of where to start when the receptionist spoke up.

"Hi, how can I do for you?"

"Hi, I'm not sure how this works," Tom said. "I spoke to a Dr. Menendez the other day?"

"No worries, are you here to visit?" She smiled up at them.

"No, we're... we're here to sign someone in," Tom said while Gideon looked at Anthony. The receptionist looked between them before turning to her computer.

"Ah, are you Anthony Russo? Dr. Menendez told me we were expecting you today. Okay, I'm going to have you sign these forms, you can take a seat and I'll have Dr. Menendez come out."

Gideon took the clipboard of forms while Tom had Anthony's carry-on. They sat beside Anthony, watching him sign away his freedom for the next few months. A man in khakis and a knit sweater came over, followed by a security guard. The man was short, stout, with a calm smile on his face, hands folded in front of him.

"Hi, there. I'm Dr. Menendez, you must be the Russos."

Tom stood and shook his hand. "I'm Tom, this is my nephew Gideon, and this is my son, Anthony."

"Pleasure. We'll need to go through Anthony's bag to make sure there isn't any contraband, and once he's finished signing, you can say your goodbyes. We'll need to do the intake interview and medical diagnosis. Anthony's doctor transferred his records over, correct?"

"Yeah, they confirmed yesterday."

"Wonderful," Dr. Menendez said, taking the clipboard from Anthony. "Alright, we'll be over here. Take your time." He and the guard took the bag and stood beside the desk, speaking to the receptionist in hushed but friendly voices.

Gideon stood, shoving his hands in his pockets,

shuffling his feet. Counted the seconds as Tom rose, slowly, each of them watching Anthony. His cousin sat and stared forward.

"Hey, bud," Tom whispered. "It's... time."

Anthony raised his face, tears in his eyes. He stood, balancing on one leg while Gideon pulled him into a tremendous hug. Gideon held his cousin, his bandmate, his brother, felt his shaking shoulders, the bony mass that was his family. Knowing when he saw him next, Anthony would be healthier and — hopefully — happier. Gideon pulled back and held him at arms length. They looked at one another and smiled.

"Thanks man," Anthony said, wiping the tears from his face. He turned to his dad, and Gideon stepped closer to the door to give them space. He heard their muffled sobs, watched as Anthony clung to his father. Tom pulled back, holding Anthony's forehead to his. Gideon watched Tom say something before planting a quick kiss on Anthony's lips, detaching himself from the only life raft he'd ever had.

They didn't look back as they walked out of the building, crunching along the gravel to the car.

Gideon cleared his throat. "Hey, want me to drive home?"

Gideon looked over at Tom, who nodded and climbed into the passenger side. Gideon was thankful to have his presence, and his mind went to Ella and her mom. How many times they'd done this and wondered if Ella had been alone each time. The thought that she probably had been broke his heart, realizing just how much strength she possessed. He was grateful she'd held her ground, pushing him to be the best version of himself.

He started the car, ready to move into the next phase of their lives.

33

Ella took a sip from her wine glass, half-listening to the rom-com on the television screen. Rachel and Julie's comments made her smile. They responded to each other quickly, hardly leaving room to butt in. Ella didn't mind too much; it was more entertaining than the actual movie. After their brilliant idea last Girl's Night for live-tweeting movies on Monday nights, they'd wanted to start the initiative with a modern classic: How to Lose a Guy in 10 Days. Next week they'd choose a bad rom-com to fill their feeds with comments resembling Mystery Science Theater 3000. It was a fun way to engage their few followers and to bring in new ones.

Her phone buzzed, and Gideon's name popped up on the screen. Her heart ached at the sight; they hadn't seen each other in a couple of weeks. Eternal Youths was busy with band practice, trying to get their new guitarist up to speed, and Gideon and Tom had just put Anthony in rehab. Ella herself had a different concert to attend every weekend, and during the week was in the midst of contacting different platforms for articles and write-ups. Word spread quickly, and Maven Media was regularly getting inquiries from potential clients. Their new hire, Ruby, was a fast learner, and Rachel was already talking about finding an HR rep and a new publicist for the music side of things. Things were looking good.

Even if Julie still had an attitude that Ella couldn't place the cause for.

Her phone buzzed again. Gideon. She smiled and sent a quick response. They could go back and forth for hours, so they usually ended up in a phone call instead. Which he'd just asked her to do. She bit her lip, debating if she could dip out of the comments and Twitter fest that she already wasn't really participating in. She knew he was having a hard time with the Anthony stuff; Rachel and Julie would probably understand a quick call. Ella unfurled from the sectional, throwing the blanket from her lap beside Julie.

"I'll be right back," Ella said, leaving the room before they could respond.

She closed her bedroom door, the other line already ringing. She still felt giddy at the thought of his voice. Ella could picture his smile, the way his dark hair fell in his eyes.

"Hey, darlin'."

Ah, the magic she'd been waiting for.

"Hey, handsome. I don't have long but wanted to check in."

"Oh, got a hot date?"

She heard the smile in his voice and laughed. "I wish. It's Girl's Night, we're live-tweeting our movie comments on the Maven Media account."

He laughed. "Sounds like you're the queen of mixing business with pleasure."

"You know it. But before I go, how are you?"

She listened to his breathing on the other end, waiting for his response.

"Eh, you know." His voice was quiet. "Honestly... I don't know how you did it so many times. How you continue to do it."

His admission made her heart catch in her throat. She knew where he was coming from. She remembered the pain of growing up with her alcoholic mom. She remembered when she was eighteen how that pain had disappeared. Or, rather, she'd become detached from it. It was just a thing to do, a task to check off every so often. But she'd never had an acknowledgment of it.

"I... You just do it, ya know? It does get a little easier, I promise." She raised her eyes to the ceiling, trying to keep the tears from spilling. "With any luck, this will be his only time."

"Yeah, here's hoping. How are you?"

Ella blinked, taking a couple deep breaths. "I'm good, same ol' stuff. We're looking into hiring more people, which will help with the workload. And we're starting this live-tweeting thing, which is fun so far. But I do have to get back to that. I can't wait to see you this weekend."

"Me neither, Ella. Thanks for calling, it was nice to hear your voice. I love you."

"I love you, too."

She hung up, staring at her phone. There was no feeling quite like having half of your heart so far away from you. Sighing, Ella shuffled back to the living room. The last thing she wanted was to see someone else's happily ever after, but duty called.

Rachel and Julie were laughing on the sectional, glasses full beside their empty plates. They looked up as Ella came into the room, their faces falling a little.

"Everything okay?" Rachel asked.

"Yeah, just needed to check in about Anthony. They brought him to rehab last week. All good though." She refilled her own glass before leaning back, cocooning herself in the blanket again.

"Hey, Ella?" Julie cleared her throat, and Ella looked at her. "Do you... Do you think for Girl's Night you could... not call Gideon? At least going forward. We never get to see you and it'd be nice to have one day when he's not around."

Rachel sipped from her glass, not looking at them. Ella blinked, processing what her best friend had just asked.

"Ummm. Like, never talk to him on the phone for Girl's Night?"

Julie nodded. "Yeah, I just... I want to spend time with you, like we used to. And I think it's fair to ask him for one night when he's not around."

Ella's mouth opened but she closed it, not knowing what to say. It felt like a ridiculous thing for Julie to ask, but Rachel's silence came as an agreement with the request. Julie went back to the movie, a heavy weight now throughout the room. Ella took a sip of the bitter liquid, gathering her thoughts.

"I don't really know why it's an issue if I need to call my boyfriend — who I only see once every two or three weeks — for five minutes to make sure everything's okay. Especially after his cousin just went to rehab and he's about to go on tour for four months."

Okay, that sounded reasonable.

"Um, because you talk to him all the time and we never get to hang out with you?" Julie faced Ella, her face red and eyes glassy. "I think it's fine to tell him you have plans on Monday nights, and then call him after. Besides, he's been a train wreck since you met him. If you save your phone calls for every big thing you need to 'check in' on, you'll be on the phone with him every night." Julie turned back to the TV, letting her words hang in the air.

"Wow, Jules. Wow. That's low, even for you. It's not my fault you accidentally fell in love with his cousin who couldn't — no, didn't — want to get his shit together. At some point you need to let it go and move on. Don't stomp on my happiness since you can't find your own." Ella couldn't stop herself. She was shaking, her breathing heavy as she realized what she'd just said.

"Fuck you, Ella." Julie said it softly before rising,

taking her wine glass to her room. Her exit was followed by a slam.

Rachel let out a sigh. "You guys take cat fight to another level." Ella could barely see Rachel glance at her, no thanks to the tears threatening to fall.

"I just... It felt like that came out of nowhere and she had no right to be mad."

"You... could've just said that, El. That was harsh. You guys both went overboard but I do think you took it too far." Rachel's voice was calm, a change of pace from her usual business-like intensity. Her hand rested on Ella's knee. "Look, we just want to spend time with you. I think it's okay to tell Gideon you have Girl's Nights on Mondays — he'll understand. I also get where you're coming from, and that the distance is hard and you guys have a lot going on. But a phone call can wait until after the movie, especially since the movie thing is also going to double as a business move. I think Julie — and myself — are just looking for a little more of a balance. That's all."

The pressure finally won, and Ella felt the tears slip down her cheeks. She thought she'd had a handle on her workload and the distance, balancing Gideon with herself and her life in the city. But her explosion with Julie said otherwise. Rachel's hand patted her knee.

"I'm sorry. I'm going to check on her real quick. I love you both, dearly, and obviously, you guys need to fix this."

Ella stared forward, hearing a knock on the door and the soft click of it shutting as Rachel entered Julie's room. Ella let the tears fall, enjoying the release she didn't know she needed.

34

Jack cradled Gideon's guitar. The young fill-in for Anthony knew an expensive guitar when he saw one, let alone played one. Gideon appreciated that, and he appreciated even more how far Jack had come since using a guitar that was set up properly. Aside from how muddy his playing had once been, he'd initially had trouble memorizing the tour set list, having only memorized two songs from the album. But the increased practices over the last couple of weeks had gotten him to have the whole EP and half the album under his belt; practice so far was going smoothly. Gideon had dropped lyrics to two songs on the table, and everyone had flocked to the new material. Even Tom seemed in better spirits than Gideon had seen in awhile. It'd been about a week since they'd dropped Anthony off, and Tom had dived into his work as Eternal Youths' manager, scheduling a couple extra practices and starting talks with Nate about hiring Maven Media for the upcoming tour.

Which they still had to talk to the rest of the band about.

But Gideon wanted to wait to have that conversation until Nate responded; no need to stir the pot if having Ella on tour wasn't even an option. He watched the guys read through the lyrics he'd dropped on the table, watching Tom's face for a reaction. Gideon had written one of the new songs for his mom and one for Anthony. He was excited at the prospect of new singles and the new direction for the next album. Having himself and his relationship with Ella more settled enabled him to explore aspects of songwriting outside of love. He hoped to create music that touched on real-world issues, music that talked about life as it was.

He was also hoping the progress with the band would mean they could cut back on practices.

The room was quiet as they read, Tom nodding his head and Ryan pacing.

"How did you hear these, Gid?" Max called out from across the room, perched on a stool with his sax around his neck. His dreads were knotted on top of his head, a blazer over a beat-up concert tee. The others looked up.

Gideon bit his lower lip. "Well, *Collapse* I wanted to be a piano piece, but I know Ant was our pianist and no one here can get past Mary Had a Little Lamb. And *Lavender* I'm not really sure. I want it to be soft but also light and fun? That one might be a little more sax heavy. I dunno, any thoughts? I'm open to anything."

"Oh, piano for *Collapse* would be cool," Lucas said from behind his drums. "I take it Ant isn't allowed a keyboard in rehab? We could have him create something."

Gideon looked at Tom, not actually sure if musical instruments were allowed.

Tom sighed and crossed his arms. "Even if he was, he's detoxing for the next month. And he's not allowed a cellphone or visitors until after that. We're on our own for this, guys."

"What if," Gideon started to say, still thinking out the timeline. "What if we focus on all the other songs first and save that one for last. We leave in five weeks, and he has three left on his detox. That leaves two weeks for us to get something together. If he's allowed or even able to. But if not, that's fine. We'll have other songs, and I'll try to keep the songs band-based."

"In the meantime, if we needed keyboard, do you think we could just copy one of his loops from old songs?" Ryan asked, grabbing his bass.

"Probably. Hey, Gid? How many more songs do you think you can get us?"

"Not sure, at least a couple. But we also don't want to give away too much of the second album on tour — no one will buy the album when it drops." Gideon picked up his guitar.

"True," Tom said. "Okay. Cool. So in the next few weeks we'll be tightening up the EP and the first album, finalizing the set list, and playing with three new singles. In three weeks we'll revisit the fourth single. Sound good?"

Gideon felt his heart sink. "I take it that means we're keeping the extra practices?" He saw the guys glance at one another before resting on Tom, who straightened his posture and looked at each of them.

"Yes. We're leaving in five weeks. We need to show 4AD we were a good bet, that we have our shit together and can not only sell well, but can also roll with the punches and perform. The… accident, made them nervous. This is our chance to wipe that away."

The guys looked dejected, murmuring their acceptance of the continued practice schedule. Gideon knew it might've been too good to be true if Tom had let some of the dates go. But he thought it'd be more likely than having 4AD agree to them hiring Maven Media and bringing his girlfriend on tour with them.

Now he had no choice but to hope for that outcome; he didn't think he could survive the four month tour not seeing Ella.

35

Julie's door was ajar, and Ella stood before it, working up the courage to open it a little further.

She'd thought about their blowup, what she'd asked for and what Julie had asked for. Rachel had been right; they both took things too far. But Ella had crossed a line, throwing Julie's pain in her face. Since Monday night, Ella had tried to figure out why those words, those emotions, had flown out under pressure. Perhaps it was underlying feelings of being judged for finding something Julie had normally rejected. Perhaps it was a sense of fear that Julie had been right and Ella wasn't doing a good job of balancing her life. Perhaps it was a bit of anger at wanting Julie to understand where she was coming from.

Either way, Ella had settled on her actions being

based out of fear instead of love. And so now she faced the door of her best friend.

She raised her hand, pausing before rapping softly against the frame. When Julie didn't answer, Ella tried a little louder.

"What?"

Rachel was out on a dinner date; Julie knew it was Ella. And her tone reflected that.

"Can I come in, Jules?"

Silence.

"Please?" Ella tried not to roll her eyes. Julie would make this more difficult than it needed to be, even though Ella knew Julie should be begging for her forgiveness.

"Fine." It came out with a huff.

Ella pushed the door open, peering in before taking a couple hesitant steps into the room. Julie sat on her bed, a book in her lap.

"What? I really don't want to talk to you."

Ella closed the door behind her and sat at the foot of Julie's bed. She tried not to smile at the contradiction Julie posed, inviting her in but telling her she didn't want to talk. It made her feel a bit better, like their friendship was strong enough to survive this hiccup with a calm conversation and honesty. Ella took in her friend's pout, her crossed arms, her eyes still trained on the pages of the book.

"I'm sorry about the other night," Ella said.

"Thank you."

Of course it was going to be like pulling teeth.

"We should probably... discuss... why we said the things we said."

"I don't think we need to. It's fine."

Jesus Christ. Ella took a deep breath, repositioning so she was facing Julie. Who finally raised her eyes to meet Ella's.

"But it's not fine, Jules. I think we both said some things, and we should talk about it calmly and honestly — and sober."

Julie's eyes shifted back to her book before she sighed and set it aside, sitting up to mirror Ella's cross-legged position.

"Fine. You really want to talk about shit? Let's." Julie's wide eyes stared at Ella's. "I feel like Gideon is still a train wreck waiting to happen. I don't trust him, Ella. And I just feel like I'm waiting for the other shoe to drop — again — because I'm always the one that has to pick up the pieces. I love you and I will always pick them up, but at this point I feel like you're just asking to get your heart broken. And yeah, I do feel like you've been letting your friendships slide. When was the last time you talked to Ben? I feel like I don't know what's up with your mom, or how your side of work is going. Hell, you don't even know what's happening in my life. All I wanted was one night where we had your attention since it's *always* about Gideon."

Julie's face was red, her breathing a step below panting. Ella waited, letting Julie calm down before addressing what she said.

"Okay." Ella nodded, still processing. She knew Julie and Gideon weren't the best of friends, but she hadn't realized Julie was on eggshells. "I completely agree with the friendships part. I've been thinking about it this past week, and you're right. As for Gideon... I thought you guys were friendly?"

Julie snorted. "Seriously? You think I *want* to be friendly with him? I do it because I know he — for whatever reason — makes you happy. And you guys are together and probably going to get married. But I think he's a mistake, El."

Ella blinked at her friend. "You don't need to be quite so harsh, Jules. I understand his past is messy, but he's been sober almost a year and his actions speak louder than words. What I don't understand is why you can't let it go, when he's only fucked up once two years ago. Does that mean every person who's made a mistake has a two year hold until they can be forgiven?"

"Oh, please. Don't be so dramatic. I think Gideon's in a bit of a different ball game given how all that shit went down."

"So where does that leave Anthony?"

Julie's mouth was left hanging, no sound coming out.

"Seriously, Jules. If you love Anthony — which I think you do but refuse to admit — it's not very fair to give him a pass. Especially since he's still in a hole he's only dug deeper. At least Gideon has been out of the hole for awhile."

Julie's mouth closed and she stared at Ella, her eyes getting glassy.

"Okay. You're right. About all of it. I wanted a casual thing while I was finishing law school, and I fell in love with your boyfriend's best friend. It got worse once we ended the physical aspect but stayed friends. But I think you know better than anyone how hard it is to remove a person from your heart, especially when you're both broken." Ella watched her wipe a couple stray tears and felt a couple of her own slip.

"I do know. But you don't take that out on me. You talk about it, you let people in. You're right, I don't know what's happening in your life. But you don't really talk about it, either. I don't care if it's about work or a date or Anthony, two years after you guys dated. I don't care if it's about your parents harping on you about getting married and having a family now that you have a job, or if it's about a cute dog you saw on the sidewalk. You know I'm always here for you, Julie." Ella watched Julie's lower lip tremble. "Girl, if you start sobbing, I'm going to start sobbing. Please don't."

That made Julie laugh, more tears escaping. "Sorry. I love you and I'm sorry." She leaned in to give Ella a hug. Ella squeezed her friend, thankful they could have an honest conversation. Even if it hurt. When she pulled away, Ella wiped her own tears away.

"Okay. So I'll tell Gideon no more calls during Girl's Night on Mondays. You'll be more open about Gideon. And we'll actually talk about things again. Deal?"

"Deal," Julie said, sniffling. She let out a heavy breath. "Can we order Chinese or something? I'm starving."

Ella smiled.

36

Gideon tried to catch Amy's eye. She'd walked into the meeting late, taking a seat on the other side of the room instead of the saved seat beside Gideon. After the way the last meeting had ended — with her being judgmental and him storming out — they had a lot to talk about.

If Joe would ever shut up and end the meeting.

Everyone clapped at something he said, and finally Gideon saw Amy stand up. Everyone followed suit, heading towards the refreshment table in the back of the room. Gideon joined the mob, hoping to grab a couple doughnuts before they disappeared. Amy was busy talking to someone anyway, and Gideon didn't want to interrupt unless it was a group. Less personal that way.

The coffee was a bit stronger this week and

paired well with the waxy chocolate coated rings of sugar Gideon loved so much. He could never figure out who brought them, but when the desserts showed up, it usually made the meeting more worth it. He nibbled one of the doughnuts, trying to find his short sponsor in the crowd. She'd moved on from the one-on-one and was in a group, laughing. Gideon swallowed his bite, adding one more doughnut to his plate before moving through the crowd to join her.

He walked up, sipping his coffee. The group's conversation faltered — he wasn't one to join conversations — but the group eventually resumed whatever he had walked into. Gideon turned to Amy.

"Hey, Ames. How's it going?" He bit into one of his doughnuts, his gaze never leaving her face.

"Pike," she said, not looking at him.

"How's it going?"

"Fine. How are you?" She glanced at him quickly.

Gideon nodded. "It's good. Anthony's been in rehab for over a week, band practices are going really well and we have a couple new songs."

"Cool. How's... Ellen? Elly?"

Oh. Petty.

Gideon cocked his head, seeing a side of Amy he hadn't seen before.

"Ella? She's great. I'm seeing her tomorrow. What's new with you?"

Amy turned to him. "You know what, Gideon? I can't do this anymore. I think you should find another sponsor."

"Wait, what?" Gideon just stared at her.

She looked away and crossed her arms. The rest of the group dropped off their conversation, some awkwardly staring and others saying their goodbyes, stepping away from the palpable tension.

"I don't think our relationship is healthy anymore and... I'm moving to Nashville next month." She shifted on her feet, looking up at him. "I'm glad I was able to help you, and I thank you for helping me. I think we both learned a lot from each other." Amy stuck out her hand, but Gideon could only stare at it. Her words were bouncing around in his head, and he was trying to grab hold of them, any of them, to make sense of what they meant.

She didn't want to be his sponsor.

Their relationship was unhealthy.

She was moving to another state.

Amy stuck her hand closer to him, and he shook it in a haze. "I... Wow, Ames. I'm really sorry you feel that way. Did I do something? I thought we were friends." Gideon couldn't hide the hurt, the disappointment, in his voice. Amy had been such a huge part of his life for almost a year. She'd picked up the phone at 3 a.m., met him at diners when all he wanted was a bottle of whiskey, had helped him fix almost every relationship with the people in his life.

"It's just time for us to move on, Gideon. I probably won't see you again, but I wish you the very best." With that, Amy turned around, throwing on her jacket as she left the church.

Gideon watched her leave, the shock of her words sinking in. Not knowing why she'd suddenly turned her back on him. He put on his own jacket, a hollow feeling in his stomach as he left the church. He'd known friends could just up and leave; he just hadn't thought his sponsor would be one of those people.

37

Flight of the Purple Birds had decided confetti was a grand idea to end their most recent show with, and Ella pulled a yellow piece out of her hair while she watched the venue workers sweep the leftovers into piles, some pieces stuck to the floor by spilled drinks. The band was loading up their van behind the venue, Paul and Everett talking with the sound engineer in the corner by the bar. It'd been another sold-out show, and Ella had been able to talk to a couple local publicists covering the event. She'd heard a label rep had been there, but she hadn't been able to catch a name or which label they belonged to, let alone talk with them.

Maybe next time.

Ella shuffled through the doors separating the merch area from the dance floor, heading towards the backstage area in the back, stopping in her tracks at the sound of her mother's gravelly laugh.

No.

She turned around and, sure enough, there stood Margaret Davis, laughing with the coat check girl, a tall man with lanky hair on her arm.

"Mom?" Ella tried to swallow the lump in her throat. Why the *fuck* was she here? Had she been drinking? Was that Jax? The questions stormed her brain as she stared at her mom, who was beaming and making her way over, pulling the man behind her while he hung as far back as possible.

"Ella!" Margaret practically bowled her over with the impact of her hug. She smelled like how Ella remembered — ylang ylang, vanilla, and patchouli — plus the soft wave of cigarettes. When she pulled back, her smile — the real one, not the acting one — took up her face. And her eyes were clear.

"What... What are you doing here?" Ella couldn't hide her surprise, glancing at the man behind her mom who was awkwardly looking around and avoiding eye contact.

"Oh, you remember Jax, right?" Her mom ignored the question, turning to pull her beau into the conversation. He gave a half smile and his hand, which Ella returned before addressing her mom again.

"I was in the city visiting Richard!" She patted Ella's arm and laughed. "He finally sent me a script and it felt good. You weren't exactly thrilled the last time I came down so I didn't want to impose, but when I heard that bird band you work with was playing, I thought I'd stop in and say hi. And Jax, of course, came along for the ride." Margaret gave Jax the sweetest smile Ella had ever seen, and she wanted to gag at the stars practically bursting from her mom's eyes at the guy in front of her.

Ella looked between the two of them, still in shock over the change in events.

"Excuse me, are you... Are you Margaret Davis?" Ella turned to find Paul staring, starstruck, at her mother. Ella felt the air around Margaret change from mom to actress as she put on her best camera smile and waltzed over to Paul.

"I'm so sorry, I didn't mean to take you from your conversation. I just... Wow. I just... I remember your movies, they always made me laugh. I... What a lovely surprise to have you here, I'm the manager for Flight of the Purple Birds. Paul. You can call me Paul." Ella watched how Paul was falling apart, stumbling over his words and vigorously shaking her mom's hand while they laughed.

"I was just stopping in to say hi to my daughter."

Paul stared, wide-eyed, between the two of them. Ella gave him a small smile, shuffling on her feet and wishing she could be invisible. Almost like Jax, who was basically mimicking her.

"Wait... I thought you were Ella Thompson?"

Ella moved to speak. "I—"

"Ella Thompson?" Margaret spun to look at Ella, hurt drawn all over her face before she turned back to Paul. "That right there is Ella Davis, my one and only. I'm sorry she told you different."

"Oh." Paul stared at them for a moment before regaining his composure. "Well, I'm sorry to have interrupted, I'll be heading out. Thanks again, Ella. Tonight was great." He nodded at her and kissed Margaret's hand goodbye before leaving Ella to face the disappointment of her mom.

"What was that?"

Yep. And so it begins.

Ella sighed. "I use Thompson for business. I want to make a name for myself since your name's so public. That's all."

"Hm. Fine." Her mother's heeled booties clicked

as she walked past Ella, pulling Jax against her. He was still a good foot or so taller than her.

"So, mom, why are you here?" Ella crossed her arms, wanting nothing more than to leave. It was late and she still had to fight with the subways to get back home.

"I told you, kid. I wanted to say hi. And introduce you to my boyfriend." Margaret raised her lips and Jax obliged. And they kissed some more. And some more, smiling the longer they went on.

Ella looked around, trying to pretend what she'd seen hadn't actually happened. Trying to forget she'd heard the word boyfriend.

"Mom," Ella said, thankful when they stopped. Jax looped his arm in front of Margaret's chest, holding her close. "I've met Jax before." Ella's eyes met his, and he smiled.

"I'm surprised you remember. You were young. What, ten?" His voice was way deeper than Ella remembered. But it was kind, and she was thrown a little from the softness it carried.

"Twelve."

She still didn't trust him.

His smile grew. "That's right, we went to mini-golf for your birthday. You didn't care so much about the putting as you did the ice cream."

A memory launched itself to the front of her mind. Ella did remember blowing out a candle in a cup of bubblegum ice cream and then picking the bubble gum pieces out of the ice cream for later. And she remembered Jax had been the only guy her mom had dated that had given her a present. She just couldn't remember what it was, thanks to her cynical twelve-year-old self thinking he was only trying to buy her affection.

"Yeah, the bubble gum ice cream was the only kind that actually had bubble gum in it."

"That's right."

"Well, I'm so glad you guys are getting on again. We're gonna dip out, honey, but it was nice to see you."

Margaret pulled Ella into a tight hug, kissing her cheek.

Ella couldn't remember the last time her mom had kissed her.

Jaxton waved as they walked out of the venue, calling their goodbyes to everyone they passed. Ella watched them leave. Maybe she'd been wrong. Maybe Jaxton was actually a kind person. Maybe he was good for her mom. Ella hugged herself, thinking that maybe — finally — her hopes were finally coming true.

38

Gideon rapped the secret knock on his mom's door, leaning against the doorjamb. Amelia threw the door open, beaming through her mess of wild curls going every which way. Ah, yes. Beautiful chaos.

"Hi, monkey," she said, pulling him into a tight hug before stepping aside for him to enter. Gideon was always so relieved when he spoke to or visited his mom. There was only one other person he'd ever met that carried almost as much sunshine as she did.

"I'm sorry it's early, I promised Ella we could go to lunch. But I know you wanted to see me." He followed is mom down the hallway, stepping into the brightly lit living room. The early morning sunlight cast gold shadows along the walls; Gideon felt like he was inside a fire.

"Oh, no worries at all! I'm usually up by now anyway. This is just an even better way to start the day." She gave him a wide smile before moving about the kitchen, getting the tea supplies together. One thing he would never understand was her attachment to tea instead of coffee, which he desperately needed. He took a seat at the island, watching her flutter about, her sheer robe waving around her, her black leggings and oversized shirt a staple. She might've gotten up around that time, but Gideon had to wake up at an ungodly hour to make it to his mom's before heading to Ella's. The thought of a nap wrapped in Ella's arms was enough to send his eyes drifting close.

"Hey!" His mom snapped her fingers in front of his face and he started. She smiled and set his chosen mug in front of him, along with honey and lemon juice. "Sorry you're so tired. But I felt it was important for us to chat, and I wasn't sure when we'd get another chance given your schedule."

Gideon watched her move about, placing an Earl Grey tea bag in his mug and a rose one in hers before rummaging in one of the cabinets while the water boiled. She returned with several boxes of tea biscuits, setting them before him. The kettle whistled behind her, and she whirled around.

"So, Gideon." She looked at him over their steaming mugs, newly filled. "Ella's a doll."

He broke into a grin. "She's something else, right?"

"I adore her." His mom sipped her tea. "How sure are you she's *the* one?"

"She's it, ma. No one else could possibly be it." He held her gaze, wanting her to know how serious he was.

She nodded. "I thought as much. Wait here." She stood and headed down the hallway.

Gideon grabbed a cookie, giving it a good dunk before biting into it. The apartment was silent aside from his chewing; he didn't know where his mom went or what she was doing, but at least she'd left the cookies. He grabbed another one, looking around. Trying to imagine what a shared apartment with Ella would look like. Gideon thought it'd be similar to what was before him, lots of light and warm colors, mixed patterns and materials.

"Sorry about that." His mom shook him from his daydream, her hands behind her back. She took a deep breath and sat on her stool. "Okay. So you're a hundred million percent sure she's the one?" Her blue eyes pierced his.

"One hundred million percent." He raised his hand. "Scout's honor."

"Okay." She brought her hands forward, opening one. A diamond ring sat in her palm. Gideon's heart clenched, realizing what it was. What she was offering. He felt the tears well, his hands clench. He looked at his mom, saw her glassy eyes and red cheeks.

"I... I know you plan on asking her to marry you. I've been saving this for you since... since your father passed." She closed her eyes, breathing through the memories. She cleared her throat before continuing. "I — obviously — wanted to meet her first. I approve, ten-fold. And I believe he would've as well. It's... it's yours, Gideon."

She took his hand, placing her engagement ring in the center before closing his fingers around it. All he could do was stare at his fist and try not to think too hard on the significance of what he held. It'd been almost twenty years since his dad had died. His mom hadn't dated since. She still choked up anytime he was mentioned. And she wanted him — and Ella — to have one of the most important pieces of their history. He allowed his tears to fall, clutching his mom's hands in his.

"Thank you."

"Of course. I know you'll take good care of it, and I always wanted a daughter. I think we'll both be lucky to have her in the family." She wiped her face and huffed. "Whew, alrighty then. Glad we got through that." She laughed. "Tell me about the band. And what your and Ella's plans are for the night. Oh, and do you know when or how you're going to propose? That's equally important as the ring." His mom sipped her tea, her bright eyes the only indication she'd been upset.

He dunked another cookie, fingering the ring in one hand while he told her all the details, getting even more excited at the prospect of asking Ella Davis to marry him.

39

"I cannot believe girls actually don't just see the writing on the wall — he's just not that into you, girl. MOVE ON!" Julie yelled at the TV, sending Ella and Rachel into hysterics. Their live-tweeting movie night was picking up followers, and despite it turning into a work event, Ella was beginning to look forward to it each week. It helped that Gideon had stayed that weekend. She'd left her phone on the island so as to not be tempted to respond to his texts, but telling him Mondays were off-limits for calls had been easier than she thought. She'd missed having a night that was all about her girl friends, and Gideon loved that she was taking time for herself and her life outside of them.

And he made it known with the things he did with his tongue.

Ella smiled at the thought, taking another sip of wine. The three of them were curled on the sectional, Pollack nestled in Rachel's lap, leftover Mexican food sitting on the coffee table.

"Oh, speaking of music events," Rachel said, nodding towards the scene in the movie. "El, I heard your mom showed up on Friday?"

Goddamnit.

"Ugh, yeah. Who'd you hear that from? Paul?" Ella shook her head, taking a healthy gulp from her glass. She wanted just one thing for herself, but her mom just couldn't let her have it.

Rachel nodded. "Yeah, her and some guy? How was that?"

Ella rolled her eyes. "That's Jax. They dated when I was twelve. He's apparently been sober for ten years and she seems happy, so I guess we'll see." Ella thought about that night, the way her mom had looked at him. "Actually, she seems head over heels. I think it's too much, too soon. But also, as long as she stays sober, I really can't care too much." She stared at the movie, trying to believe the words she'd said.

"Huh. That's kind of odd, him coming back now that she's sober," Rachel said, still watching the movie.

"Maybe." Ella shrugged. "Maybe she thought he was the one that got away and reached out to him first. We don't really talk about that stuff." Her wine was a comfort, especially while she watched the cringeworthy behavior of the girl onscreen, desperate for the guy's attention.

"This is just painful. Do any of us do this?" Julie refilled her glass, shaking her head.

Rachel laughed. "Kill me if I ever do. Please."

"You know what else you can kill me over? Hearing Ella and Gideon." Julie shuddered and laughed. "Like... Damn, girl. Glad you're happy but please just... Ya know..." She raised her eyebrows, taking another drink.

Ella looked at her friend, wide-eyed. "No... No, I'm so sorry! I thought we were quiet." She hid her face behind her hands, the girls laughing beside her.

"Hey, I get it. If my fiancé looked like that, I wouldn't want to be quiet either." Julie's laugh rang out, but she was the only one. Ella froze, turning to face her, Rachel staring at both of them.

"Wait... What?" Ella's voice sounded foreign to her.

"I..." Julie closed her mouth and turned to the TV. "What?"

"Julie... What do you mean 'fiancé?'" Rachel leaned forward, trying to get in Julie's line of sight.

"Nothing. Forget I said anything." She kept her glass by her mouth, sipping from it without looking at either Rachel or Ella.

Ella stared at her best friend. "Julie, what do you know?"

The words lingered before Julie sighed. "I've said far too much. Wow, this movie's really crazy. Right?" She laughed nervously, glancing at each of them before turning back to the movie.

Ella looked at Rachel, trying to decide whether to drop it or keep pushing. She could see Rachel thinking the same thing, but her friend's head shake gave her the answer she needed. Ella let the subject drop, refilling her wine glass and acting completely engrossed in the movie, her friend's comments stilted. Trying to find the flow they'd had before Julie dropped her bomb. Ella knew she and Gideon would be together, she just didn't think it'd be so soon. She figured they'd live in the same city for a bit, enjoy each other after the hectic travel months they had ahead of them. Then maybe discuss the logistics of getting engaged. Especially since she didn't want to live with someone before they were married.

But when she thought about what it was like to wake up beside him, to fall asleep to the sound of his breathing, she was disappointed they hadn't tied the knot sooner.

40

The ring weighed heavy, the velvet box Tom had given Gideon bulky in the front pocket of his jeans as he paced outside the rehearsal room. But Gideon wasn't going anywhere without that little reminder of the life he'd worked for, the life he deserved.

He could hear the rest of Eternal Youths inside, laughing and trying out different chords for one of their new singles. After visiting Ella that weekend, Gideon had gone straight to Tom's to tell him about his plan to propose. And to talk to him about his plan to move to New York City. Gideon's personal life was moving along more smoothly than he'd expected; it was time to talk to the band about what was next. Tom had understood where he was coming from and agreed they should all make the move downstate after the tour. 4AD was headquartered there, and being in the city opened up more opportunities for them all. Tom had also gotten word that Nate was open to Eternal Youths hiring Maven Media for the festival tour and would review the contracts to make sure there was nothing barring outside help.

Facing the door, Gideon took several deep breaths, shaking out his arms to release some of the building tension. The knob was cold in his hand, but he pushed through. The guys looked up as he entered, standing around with their instruments mid-conversation. Tom leaned against the far wall and threw Gideon a small smile.

"Hey, guys," Gideon said. "Did I miss anything?" He shoved his hands in his pockets, playing with his eight-month AA chip in one hand and the box in the other.

"We might have a direction for *Lavender*." Max broke into a smile. "And Lucas is a dipshit, but that's nothing new."

They all laughed, doubling over.

"Yeah, I figured as much. So, guys. I actually wanted to talk to you about some things." Gideon held his breath, waiting for his friends to compose themselves. They finally caught their breaths and stood, watching him. Tom gave him a nod.

"As you know, Ella and I have been dating for awhile. But I've always known she was the one. I'm planning on proposing before tour —"

Excited yells and congratulations filled the air, the band moving in to hug Gideon. It felt good, knowing he had their support with this tremendous life decision.

"But guys, that's not it." He was laughing at their jokes, their support, their brotherhood. But he needed to make sure they understood the consequences of this decision. For all of them.

"As you also know, she lives in New York City. I'm moving there, after the tour." Gideon looked from guy to guy, releasing the breath he'd been holding. Ryan nodded his head and Max smiled, Jack and Lucas just staring at him.

"We figured, man," Lucas said.

"Honestly, we should all probably move down there," Max added. "I have family I can stay with in the Bronx while I find a place."

Gideon felt relief wash over him. He knew the moving part would go over almost as well as planning on getting engaged. But talking to them about bringing Ella on tour was another matter.

"Cool. Awesome." He nodded, still staring at his bandmates, trying to work up the courage to keep going. Wondering if he really could have it all. "So, one more thing."

He watched as their faces grew serious, waiting for him to continue. Gideon tried to keep the plan straight in his head: go over how 4AD hadn't deliver on half the marketing items they'd promised, the logic of hiring an outside publicist, limit talk of Ella.

"I was looking over the proposed marketing plan from 4AD, and double-checking what they said would be done versus what was actually done. Turns out, they haven't delivered on half the stuff." He watched the shock take over their faces and kept going. "Apparently, we have the option to hire an outside publicity firm to fill in the blanks."

Lucas's lips quirked into a smile while Ryan narrowed his eyes. "Outside publicity firm?"

"Yeah, and I guess some publicists fall under tour operations; they go on tour and manage things like interviews, press, venue owners, booking agents, and the like." Gideon felt his heart pick up the pace, Jack looking between everyone. Even Max was trying not to laugh.

"So you think we should hire an outside publicity firm — but not just the firm, perhaps a publicist — to go on tour with us? Ya know, make sure everything's... running okay?" Ryan couldn't hide his amusement, knowing exactly what Gideon was getting at.

Gideon smiled at them, his hands feeling clammy. "Yeah, exactly. 4AD promised us certain things that they're not delivering on, but our numbers for this tour will impact how they treat our next album. We need to make the most of the situation, using everything at our disposal."

"You, uh, wouldn't happen to have a firm — or publicist — in mind, would you?" Lucas raised his eyebrows at Gideon.

"I mean, I can think of a couple..."

"Gideon, it makes sense to hire an outside firm. Especially since your girlfriend is really good at her job. I think since she knows our music inside and out, bringing her along is the only logical move. Right?" Max crossed his arms, looking at each member. They all burst out laughing.

"Yeah, basically," Gideon said.

"Dude, next time just ask." Ryan slapped his back, still laughing.

Gideon shrugged. "I just wasn't sure how you guys would feel about it."

"Gideon, if you don't know that we love and support you by now, that we one hundred and twenty thousand percent approve of Ella, you crazy."

Max shook his head, tying up his dreads. "So now that we have that settled, can we jam? I'm feeling good."

Gideon knew what he meant and couldn't wait to channel the energy he had into their music.

41

"So, Rach?" Julie called from her desk. Ella looked up, blinking to bring her friend into focus. Sorting through emails was the bane of her existence, especially the number of potential clients waiting for responses.

Rachel looked up. "What's up?"

Ella had never seen Rachel look anything other than bright-eyed and polished, but it looked like the onslaught of emails was getting to her too, based off the circles under her eyes and the slight frizz her hair boasted.

"I hate to ask… but could we please hire people?" Julie sounded desperate, and Ella couldn't blame her. While Ruby had recently started and was beginning to oversee their TV and film clients, Ella and

Rachel helped her manage those while also taking care of their music and publishing clients. Julie was not only in charge of everything related to human resources, she was also their only legal person; she was CC'd on every email in regards to contracts and needs. If Ella felt overwhelmed by the number of bands emailing her and the tour with Flight of the Purple Birds in the fall, she could only imagine how Julie felt. Or Rachel.

Rachel sighed. "Yeah... We should probably talk about that, to make sure any funds we receive from new clients line up with any new hires."

Ella watched her stare into space, thinking, knowing she was probably thinking about how to get more money without asking her father for a short-term loan. "I know we're all swamped, but if we sign the two presses, three bands, and the production company, we could double down for the next couple of weeks while we find a human resources rep and a second music publicist. Then in probably a month we could look into a second publishing publicist and maybe another legal member?" She looked at Ella, her business partner.

"I think that makes the most sense," Ella said. "Ruby is a fast learner — she should be caught up with the media clients and can probably help you with yours." She smiled at Ruby, who blushed almost as bright as her hair. "I think the HR rep is priority number one. We have some time before we need to find a music publicist. If we needed to find one for publishing first, we could. Sorry, Jules, but legal is way more expensive so we should probably hold off on that until the last possible minute."

Julie shrugged. "Hey, I totally get it. Honestly, just getting the payroll and benefits and shit off my plate will help a ton."

Rachel nodded. "Okay, great. Ruby, why don't you take the rest of the day? Whatever work you need to do, you can do from home."

"R-really? I mean, are you sure?" Ruby, despite being almost thirty, sounded like a fifteen-year-old getting unexpected permission from her parents to go to a party.

"Yes, seriously." Rachel laughed. "Honestly, I'd prefer if everyone could work from home but I don't think we'd be as productive. But this is part of owning our own thing — doing what we want. Enjoy the rest of your day." She turned to Julie while Ruby gushed 'thank you' and packed her bag. "Why don't you come over here, Jules. You can help me with the job posting since I'm not entirely sure what you need. Ella, I'm assuming we can rework the posting for the TV and media publicist and use it for music?"

Ella felt a weight lift from her shoulders. "Yeah, just send me what you posted for that and I'll rework it."

Fucking finally. Every morning Ella felt like she was drowning when she checked her work email. Since Maven Media had agreed to tour publicity for one client, they now had to offer it to others. Not everyone wanted to pay for that service, but it still meant that when Ella was out at a show or traipsing across the country, she couldn't work on her other clients.

"Bye, guys! See you tomorrow." Ruby waved and dipped out, taking some of the cheery energy of the office with her. Ella was so pleased she was the person they'd hired; Ruby was not only a fast learner, but she was uneasily fazed and always smiled.

Ella's email dinged with the job posting Rachel had written before, and she opened it while Julie scooted her chair beside Rachel's. Editing was always more enjoyable than answering emails or scheduling phone calls, especially when the finished product would help make her life a million times easier. She read the post, smiling at how easy this was going to be, popping in her headphones to get started.

42

Gideon glanced at the clock on Tom's oven, pacing around the island. Tom sat with his phone on the counter, waiting for Nate's call to come through.

"Gideon, relax." Tom's voice was mellow, and it did help Gideon slow down. A little.

"Seriously, take a seat. If he says no, we'll figure out what's next. But considering it'd help them make money, I highly doubt that'll be the answer."

Gideon sighed, plopping onto the stool across from his uncle, resting his arms on the counter.

"Okay. Okay." He glanced at the clock as the phone rang.

"Hey, Nate. Good to hear from you." Tom sounded strong, friendly.

Nate's voice crackled on the other end. "Hey, Tom, thanks for finding time for a quick call. I reviewed the contract 4AD has with Eternal Youths, and there's nothing that prohibits the use of an outside publicist. However, just note that 4AD will not cover any costs, and, obviously, any publicity done that increases the band's sales will still be split by the contractual agreement. No extra percentages for you guys."

Tom pursed his lips.

"Totally understand," Tom said. "What are the rules surrounding using your contacts or outlined plan versus our own?"

"How do you mean?"

"Well, your proposal included a write-up in Rolling Stone. Let's say our person includes that in their plan. Would they be able to use your contacts? Is it okay if their plan includes items off of yours that weren't delivered on?"

Nate was silent for a moment. Gideon met Tom's eyes over the phone, waiting.

"A good question. You cannot use our contacts but if you feel we did not meet your expectations, they can use their own contacts to deliver on any plan they set forth."

Tom tried not to laugh at the political answer Nate had provided while Gideon tried to keep himself from pacing the room.

He couldn't believe his ears. What a rip-off.

"Okay, great. What information do you need in regards to us using a third party?" Tom scratched his forehead, his smile betraying how ridiculous he thought this was.

"Just the name of the firm and the specific publicist who ends up helping you."

"Perfect. We'll get that to you ASAP. Thanks again, Nate."

"Sure thing, have a good one."

They hung up and Tom let out a chuckle. "Un-fucking-believable."

"Seriously." Gideon's leg bounced, his head shaking. "Like, let's not do what we say we're going to, so you feel like you have to pay someone else to do it. But we're not going to help in any way, but rather take a little credit for the extra work someone else is doing."

Tom let out a sigh and looked at Gideon. "Yeah, I guess that's just how the business is. But hey, at least he approved it."

Gideon looked at Tom, his words sinking in. Nate had approved the band's use of an external publicist. And the band had given their approval to have Ella along.

43

"Hey, mom." Ella cradled the phone between her ear and her shoulder, feeding Pollack his goopy dinner.

"Hey, kid. How's it going?"

"Fine, how are you?" Ella tried not to sound annoyed. Her mom had called mid-scoop, the ring startling Ella and causing a piece of cat food to drop on her bare foot. If she didn't think about it, she wouldn't feel nauseous while she finished her baby's nightly feeding.

"Good, good, good." Ella heard the click of a lighter, the sucking in and the blowing out of her mom smoking. "It was nice to see you the other night."

Ella finished dishing, the wet spot on her skin becoming almost unbearable. "Yeah, you too. Jax is nice."

"Isn't he lovely?" She heard the smile in her mom's voice and was reminded of the way her mom had looked at him, the way he'd held her. Ella really shouldn't have been so judgmental; she knew love when she saw it. "He is, mom." Ella wiped the slime off her foot, throwing shade at Pollack while she did. Not that he cared, too consumed with his dinner to pay her any mind. "So why are you calling?"

"Jesus, kid. Can't a mom call her daughter?"

Ella shook her head. Her mom rarely, if ever, called just to chat. "Sorry, I didn't mean it like that. I'm just… in the middle of some things."

Her mom laughed her gravelly laugh. "Oh, sorry. Did I interrupt you and your man friend?"

"No, he doesn't visit during the week. I'm working." Ella wiped down the counters, giving Pollack a pet on her way to her room.

"Well, la-di-da." An inhale and an exhale. "I actually just wanted to let you know Jax was moving in."

Ella stopped at her door, the words taking her by surprise.

"Actually he already moved in," Margaret clarified when Ella didn't respond.

"I… I don't know what to say."

"I mean, a congrats? Maybe? Some sort of, 'wow,

mom! You have your shit together!' would probably be a good place to start." The steel had entered her mom's voice and Ella closed the door behind her, flopping onto her bed. Trying to decide if it was worth picking a fight or giving her mom what she craved.

Ella sighed, trying for the latter. "Wow, mom. Super happy for you, that's exciting."

"Jesus Christ, you can never be happy for me, can you?"

Ella laughed, throwing her arm over her eyes. Her mom was unbelievable sometimes. "Right, 'cause you have such a great track record. Fine. I think it's too fast. I would like to see you sober, post-rehab, for a year. No men."

"Well that's good for you but it's my life and when the one person you thought you'd lost comes back, you don't let it go." Margaret's voice cracked, and it hit Ella like a ton of bricks. She couldn't remember the last time her mom had cried, over anything. And Ella did know what that was like. Gideon was that person for her. They'd talked a lot about forgiveness and not holding the past against one another. Ella's history with her mom was a hell of a lot more complicated and a hell of a lot more tragic. But didn't the same rules apply?

"Okay." Ella let out a sigh. At some point, she'd have to work on forgiving her mom. At some point, she'd have to give her a chance to be different from the person Ella had grown up with. "Please just be careful. Have your boyfriend move in, live your life, but please don't fall into old habits."

"I wish you'd give me the benefit of the doubt, Ella."

"And I wish you'd understand where I'm coming from. Margaret."

"What, you're going to resort to being fifteen again? I didn't like that then, I certainly as fuck don't like it now."

"Why can't you see where I'm coming from? You've been in and out of rehab since I was fourteen. TWELVE YEARS, MOM. You brought all sorts of guys through the house. I had to pick up every single broken piece of you. I'm sick and tired of it, I can't keep doing it. I'm glad you're happy. Seriously. I'm just asking you to be careful. To think of me, your daughter, for once." Ella couldn't stop the words, couldn't stop the sobs from escaping. She wailed into the phone, feeling like she was five and cut herself, fifteen and going through her first heartbreak, twenty and rushing her mom to the hospital, not sure if she was going to make it. Margaret didn't say anything. But Ella could hear her breathing on the other end, and she held onto it. Centered herself around it.

Ella, heaving, fell back against her bed, curling herself into a ball while her panting subsided. She closed her eyes, matching her breathing to her mom's. They sat in silence for some time before her mom spoke, her whisper cracked but full of unshed tears.

"I... so sorry... honey." Her mom sniffled. "Thank you... for saying something. You're... right. I promise. I know I... failed, at a lot of things. But especially at being your mom."

Ella blinked, wanting to wrap her mother's words in a bow and carry them in her pocket. The words she'd always wanted, needed, to hear. The weight she'd been carrying around and the dread she'd felt anytime her mom came up eased, ever so slightly. Maybe actually saying what was on her mind was part of forgiveness. For both of them.

"You have always been the light of my life, Ella. My one and only." Her mom took a deep breath. "I know I missed a lot. But please give me a chance to not miss any more."

Ella sniffled, trying to find her voice. "I... want to,

mom. But it's going to take time. And it's going to take action. I need to see the changes."

Her mom released the breath she'd been holding. "I understand. Take all the time you need, but please give me a chance. To be there. To be your mom."

It sounded like a good place to meet in the middle. Ella still had a small piece of her that felt her mom owed her more than halfway, but maybe by showing her mom she was willing to work on forgiveness, her mom would be willing to work on really being there. Or maybe she wouldn't, and this was the mom Ella was gifted with. And maybe that was enough.

"Okay, mom. Thank you."

"Of course, honey. I have to run, but thank *you*. I love you more than anything." Her mom hung up before Ella could respond. She was left alone, the sound of her tired breathing all she had for company. And the thought that maybe — just maybe — she and her mom could have a relationship again.

44

"Monkey! What a surprise, I thought you had meetings on Fridays?"

Gideon smiled at his mom's chipper voice. "Sometimes, but I wanted to talk to you more."

"Oh, you know how to flatter me. How are you?" Rustling came from her end, followed by a bang and a clatter.

"I'm fine, are you?" He laughed, picturing his mom's crazy hair and her robe flapping around her while she tried to clean up whatever she'd dropped.

"Of course! But why are you calling me? Shouldn't you be, I dunno, out? With Ella? Not talking to your mom on a Friday night?"

"Nah, this is a perfect Friday." Gideon sat on his couch, his plate of homemade spaghetti and garlic bread in his lap. He started twirling some noodles around his fork. "I wanted to talk to you about moving. Not you, me."

She barked out a laugh. "Oh, thank god. I'm never moving again, this is it for me. What were you thinking?"

Gideon finished chewing his bite, savoring the garlic and parsley. Yeah, this was a perfect Friday, with the exception of missing Ella.

"We leave the first week of May. But practices end the last week of April. I was thinking of breaking my lease early and moving my stuff into your guest bedroom while I'm away, and then staying with you when I get back until I find a place. Ella will be on tour September to November, so you don't have to worry about... that."

She was quiet for a moment. "Have you asked her to marry you yet?"

He sighed through a mouthful of bread. "No, I'm waiting until I see her next."

"Well, what if she says no?"

"Ma, she's not going to say no."

"I mean, yeah, of course not. But what if? Best to be prepared. Will you guys be moving in together?"

"I just don't know. We'll probably wait to move in until we're married. We're both a little old-fashioned like that. And she's not going to say no."

His mom sighed on the other end. "If that's what you think is best. Have you heard about the hiring her for tour thing? You were waiting on someone for that, right?"

His food stared back at him while he took several deep breaths. Maybe calling his mom to talk about his life while he was eating wasn't such a great idea.

"Yeah, Tom's going to formally call them this week. Nate from the label said it was fine, we just have to cover costs and we don't get an extra profit percentage."

"Sounds like a load of bullshit to me," his mom huffed. "Weren't they supposed to do the things you're hiring her to do anyway?"

Gideon chuckled. "Yep. That's exactly what I said."

"Goddamn. A bunch of money-hungry losers." He heard another clatter on her end and a muffled 'shoot'.

"What are you up to tonight, ma?"

Her sigh lasted longer than necessary. "Oh, you know. Living my best life. Alone. Here, in this big ole apartment. Oh, have you heard from Anthony?"

Gideon stopped eating, his cousin's name breaking his heart.

"Nah, I think next week we get to visit. Or he gets

to call us. I'm not really sure, Tom would know." He'd have to remember to ask Tom when he got off the phone with his mom.

"Hm, okay. I'll check in with him. So, monkey, you're really not doing anything tonight?" A fork scraped against a plate, her soft chewing in his ear.

"Nope, just eating some s'ghetti. What about you?"

"Ah, me too! It was always our Friday night go-to, wasn't it?" Her voice was laced with sadness from the time when his father was still around. He'd always make spaghetti on Fridays, and they'd sit on the couch with their food while they watched a movie. Gideon thought about his mom, alone in her apartment, with her plate of spaghetti and the memory of his father.

"Hey, ma?"

"Hmm?"

"Would you maybe want to watch a movie together? We could start it at the same time, stay on the phone with each other?"

"R-really?" Her voice hitched, and Gideon's heart broke a little more. He hadn't realized how lonely his mom must've been. Gideon had been more or less absent the last decade. It was only in the past couple of years that he'd started rebuilding their relationship, and even more recently their friendship. Picturing her grieving her husband — and then her alcoholic son — by herself was almost too much to bear.

"Of course, ma. You still like action or horror movies? I know a couple really good ones."

45

Ella and Julie stood on either side of Rachel, looking at the printed out resumes. The edge of the desk was biting into Ella's hand while she leaned forward, looking at the publicist pile. Julie was in a similar position, but with the human resources applicants.

"These are doozies." Julie threw a hand into the air. "I mean, you know, they're not. They're all perfectly qualified. But what a stupid process." She waltzed back to her desk, seeming to give up altogether on the process for the time being. Ella shook her head, grabbing her pile and tapping it on the desk.

"I guess I should look through these?" Ella looked at Rachel leaning back in her chair, chestnut hair in a sleek ponytail, arms folded across her chest.

Her business partner sighed, resting her head in her hands.

"Yes, please. I sorted through them, those are our best candidates. I just can't read anymore boring resumes or weird cover letters."

Ella patted her friend's shoulders, dropping the HR applications on Julie's desk before taking a seat at hers.

After several pages, they all started to look the same. Ella looked around the office, bleary-eyed. A fast learner, Ruby was plugging away on her computer and hadn't asked a single question in at least a week. Julie had her head nestled in her arms, her resumes abandoned beside her. Rachel sat, straight as a pin, typing as fast as possible with her headphones in. Ella really needed to ask them about putting in a speaker.

The single office phone — on Rachel's desk — rang, freezing everyone. They all looked at the desk phone, the green light flashing as it rang again. Rachel looked from person to person, taking a headphone out.

"Why is someone calling our phone?"

Everyone shrugged and shook their heads. They had the office phone just to have it, putting the number on their website in case something happened with their cellphones. But so far, they'd all only ever given their personal numbers to clients, and clients had been gotten through word of mouth.

Rachel picked up the phone before it rang again, her voice betraying her confusion. "Maven Media, this is Rachel speaking. How can I help you?"

Ella watched her face. The furrow between her brows disappeared, her laugh ringing out clear. "Oh, one moment, Tom! Sorry about that, I'll put her on. Please hold." A manicured nail tapped a button and Rachel bent over laughing.

"Holy shit, it's Tom. From Eternal Youths. He said he wanted to be professional so he found our office number on the website. It's for you, Ella." Rachel shook her head, switching seats with Ella.

"Tom?" Ella was beyond confused as she pressed the phone to her ear.

"Hey! Sorry about the run around, I'm calling about a professional matter so I wanted to be... professional." He laughed. "In any case, I wanted to ask you about your rates. I downloaded the sheet on your website. As you know, Eternal Youths is going on tour this summer, from May through August."

Ella couldn't believe her ears. Had Gideon managed to have everyone sign off on her touring with them? And — even better — on hiring Maven Media?

She cleared her throat, trying to focus on the conversation. "Um, yeah. Yes. As you guys are considered friends and family, I'm sure we can work out a discount. You're looking to hire us for the festival season plus tour accommodation, correct?"

Ella turned to Rachel, mouthing what the discount would be. Rachel looked like a deer in the headlights, shaking her head. Ella could see her friend's gears turning, trying to figure out an appropriate rate as Tom confirmed and explained the tour itinerary.

"Oh, perfect." She did once last glance at Rachel.

"Half. Just tell him half," Rachel said, sighing and throwing her hands in the air.

"Okay, so Tom, we worked out we could give you a fifty percent discount on the rate. Unfortunately, all publicist travel expenses will be the responsibility of Eternal Youths."

"Wow, half? Are you sure Ella?"

"For you? Absolutely." She smiled, unable to believe this was actually happening. "I'll put you in contact with Julie, you can give her the details and she'll handle the contract."

"Great. I'll text you the email for correspondence.

Thanks, Ella. I'm excited to have you with us, I think it'll be really great for the team."

"Me too, Tom. Have a great day."

She hung up, warmth blooming through her body at the thought of being on the road, with Gideon, for so long. And getting paid to do it.

46

The mansion loomed before them, stopping Gideon in his tracks. Tom kept walking towards the entrance of Pinewood Rehab, the sound of crunching gravel echoing through the clearing in the woods.

Gideon didn't know what to expect. Anthony had been in the facility for over thirty days, detoxing from his demons. Like Gideon had last year, only without inpatient treatment. With each step he took to where Tom was waiting on the portico, Gideon tried to stuff his anxiety down. Focusing on the crunch his shoes made, the creak of the opening door.

Stepping into the waiting room, lit gold by sconces and smelling of eucalyptus, the receptionist behind the large wood desk smiled at them. "Hi, gentlemen. How can I help you?"

"We're, uh, here to visit?" Tom's voice cracked. "My son, Anthony Russo."

"Sure thing, one moment." She walked down one of the hallways, leaving Tom at the desk and Gideon looking around, hands in his pockets. It reminded him of a spa.

The woman came back. "You can follow me." She smiled and turned on her heel, leading them down the main hallway behind the desk. They shuffled behind her, glancing at one another.

"You're not going to search us?" Tom asked.

"We don't usually, especially with parents. We trust our patients and we trust their parents — there's a reason they come here, and there's a reason they pay what they do. Also, since he just finished the thirty day detox, you only have an hour. Here we are, you can take a seat anywhere."

They'd reached a small room with empty tables and chairs, the far wall filled with large windows looking out over a lawn. People in light jackets strolled around, and Gideon could see where, in the summer, the lawn would be filled with activities.

"Hey."

Gideon whipped around at the voice, Tom moving to envelop his son in a bear hug.

Despite being mostly hidden by Tom, Gideon

could make out some of the physical changes in Anthony. His skin had more color, his body not quite as bony. His eyes were squeezed shut, but Gideon bet they were clear and that the dark circles he'd had before were mostly gone.

They pulled apart, wiping their faces and chuckling about something Tom said under his breath. He stepped aside, letting Gideon and Anthony have their moment. Gideon held his cousin, thankful to have him in his life again. Thankful that Anthony felt healthy and pumped full of energy he hadn't had before.

"I missed you, man," Anthony said, giving Gideon a squeeze before standing at arms length with his hands on Gideon's shoulders.

"I missed you too, although I'm glad they finally got you to shower." Gideon cracked a smile, nodding toward Anthony's damp hair. That got a small laugh out of Anthony, which made Gideon smile even more. His cousin had his sense of humor back.

"Yeah, yeah. That was more me, I smelled dank." Anthony shook his head, still smiling, as he made his way over to one of the circular tables by the window. They all sat, looking between one another.

"So... How are things? What's new?"

Lighter topics seemed a good way to start, and

Tom and Gideon filled the air with mindless chatter. New recipes Tom was trying, a new band Gideon was listening to. The flat tire Ryan's van had gotten. A trip to a coffee shop with Ryan, Lucas, and Max. Gideon wasn't sure how much time had passed, the stories running together. He was putting off talking about anything that might hurt Anthony. Anything that might make this harder than it was. At some point, Anthony's eyes had glazed over, and Gideon found himself done grasping for conversational straws. Tom followed, and the three of them sat in silence before Anthony cleared his throat.

"How's the band? Is Jack ready?"

"Yeah, turns out the issue was his guitar. We switched it with mine and he's been doubling down on memorizing. Plus, we have a few singles from the second album we've been prepping." Gideon took a deep breath, unsure of how Anthony would feel knowing they were working on the next project.

"Wow... That's awesome." The small smile Anthony gave was a poor attempt at hiding how he felt. "I miss playing with you guys."

"We miss having you. We've been trying to find workarounds to your parts, or live versions versus studio versions, for when you're back." Tom pursed his lips. "Actually, we were thinking about asking if you wanted us to ask about letting you have a keyboard in here. We can record what we have and maybe you could work on your parts? If you're feeling up to it, of course."

Anthony's old smile came back. "That sounds like a dream. I think they'd classify that as music therapy. Maybe I could get the tour singles first and record something for you guys to use?"

"We were thinking of asking that exactly," Gideon said, feeling excited about Eternal Youths for the first time in months.

"Sweet. I'm sure Menendez won't mind." Anthony nodded, letting their conversation end. They sat in silence. Gideon wasn't sure what to say, what would hurt or what would help.

"How's... Ella?" Anthony asked, leaning back in his chair. He zipped up his hoodie, shoving his hands in his pockets.

"She's good. Um, we're —"

"We're actually hiring Maven Media for tour," Tom cut in, looking at his hands on the table, "to help make up the outreach 4AD wasn't able to do. She'll be touring with us."

Anthony stared between the two of them.

"Oh... Wow, okay. That's great. Right? She'll be

with you guys and will help with publicity stuff. Is she still living in the city?"

Gideon bit his lip, meeting his cousin's gaze. "Yeah, and, um... We're all planning on moving there after the tour."

He dropped the bomb, watching Anthony for a reaction. The old Anthony would've had everything on his sleeve. This one just sat and stared at him.

"Yeah... I wanted to talk to you about that, Ant. I think it's time for us, the band, to move to a place with more opportunity. I'll keep my house in Sugar Grove for when we need a break, but we all talked about it. The others agree, and since we'll have some time after tour before working on the second album, the timing is kind of... perfect." Tom looked at Anthony, who stared back, still not saying anything.

"And, um, also...." Gideon swallowed. "I'm planning on asking Ella to marry me. Soon, next time I see her. I... I just wanted you to know."

Anthony looked out the window and nodded. "Wow, a lot's been happening."

Gideon heard the melancholy in his voice, the understanding that he'd missed out on big moments everyone else had had.

"I take it you found a ring?"

"Yeah, Julie..." Gideon realized he probably

shouldn't have mentioned Anthony's ex and Ella's best friend, but he was too far in to stop. "Julie actually helped me at first, but after my mom met Ella, she gave me the ring my dad had given her."

Anthony tried to hide the sting Julie's name brought. "Oh, that's awesome, man. Glad to hear everything's good. Can't wait to get out of here next month so I can move on with my life like you guys have." His laugh was bitter. "So you'll bring me my keyboard if Menendez gives the go-ahead?" He ran his hands though his hair and turned back to Tom.

"Absolutely. You doing okay, Ant? How is it in here?" Tom's brow furrowed, and Gideon felt the same. Anthony was more distressed by all the news than Gideon thought he'd be.

"It's fine, everyone's pretty chill." Anthony shrugged. "Food is good, arts and crafts is kinda fun, and therapy is interesting. I hate the group shit but it's fine."

"I'm glad to hear it," Tom said as the receptionist came back.

"Hello, I'm so sorry but the hour is up." She stood by the door, looking away to give them a semblance of privacy.

Gideon looked at his cousin, seeing his face turn red.

"Well, thanks for coming guys. Be sure to ask Menendez before you leave, I'd like that keyboard sooner rather than later." Anthony stood, trying to hide the emotion in his voice. Gideon stood as well, giving his cousin a tight hug. Anthony pulled away first, hiding his face while moving to Tom. Gideon watched Anthony's shoulders shake, Tom's face scrunched up while he held onto Anthony for dear life. Gideon turned away, feeling the burn in his throat move to his eyes.

Gideon couldn't imagine what it'd be like to be on his own like Anthony was, to get a taste of the outside world, of his family, only to have it torn away. He was grateful he'd never needed to be here. Grateful he had found something — someone — that filled him with enough purpose to find the strength by himself to build the life he wanted.

47

Ella sat on her bed, looking around her room. Wondering what it'd look like if she lived with Gideon. Her phone buzzed beside her, and she smiled at a text from Gideon letting her know he was on his way from Sugar Grove. She felt the excited pit in her stomach grow. Ever since Julie had let slip he was planning on proposing, Ella couldn't help but imagine different scenarios in which he'd drop to one knee. She couldn't help but wonder if he'd do it before they left for tour, or maybe wait until after to make sure they didn't drive each other crazy. She smiled at the thought, already knowing that no matter how crazy they drove each other, they would always be together.

A text from her mom came through, a picture of a dress she thought was cute for Ella. She was out with Jax, shopping of all things. Ella responded, still wrapping her head around the person her mom had become. It was refreshing. Margaret would never be the mother Ella had needed growing up, but she was becoming a mother Ella wanted. And that was enough.

She and Julie had worked from home today since Rachel was out with a client and Flight of the Purple Birds had their last New York City show tomorrow. There were still a couple hours until Gideon showed up — and a couple left in the work day. Ella willed herself to open her laptop, to squeeze in a little more work before she could call it a day. Better yet, she should take her computer to the den, where Julie was situated. It was always easier to work when someone else was as well. Sighing, she dragged her feet to the kitchen, figuring a snack would help motivate her. Julie was sitting at the island, still in pajamas and her glasses, which she only wore if she thought no one was looking.

"Hey," Julie said. She glanced up, surprised, before returning to her screen. "I thought you were out."

Ella set her computer down across from her friend. "Hey. You're not going out tonight?"

Julie laughed. "Yeah, with all this work I have to

do? So much time to party. Look at me, a regular party animal over here."

"Hey, you never know." Ella smiled, grabbing a handful of chocolate chips from the pantry before sitting down. "Gideon's staying over tonight, FYI."

"Cool, cool. You haven't seen each other in awhile, right?" Julie looked at her over the top of her laptop.

"No, we haven't seen each other since before you let slip he was planning on proposing." Ella smirked at Julie, who rolled her eyes.

"I'm sorry, okay. I mean, you had to know it was coming at some point."

"Yeah, but also, now that I know it's going to happen but I don't know when, there's all this anxiety." Ella opened her email, scanning the subject lines.

"I totally get that and, again, I'm sorry. But at least the how will be a surprise. And the ring! It's not like you found a jewelry box in his jacket or something you know?" Julie raised her eyebrows before turning back to her computer. "Oh, did you get CC'd on those emails from the possible new hires? Looks like they're a go for interviews on Monday."

"Yeah, looking at those now. If we can find two

people in that one day, then we could hire by end of week."

"Thank fucking god." Julie sighed and shook her head. "Also, did you hear about Ben?"

Ella's head snapped up, imagining the worst. "Um, no. What happened with Ben? Is he okay?"

"Oh, shit, sorry. Didn't realize how that sounded." Julie laughed and Ella's shoulders relaxed. "Ben got a job at one of the big publishing houses. He won't tell me which one until he gets his first paycheck, but he said he'll be moving down here right after graduation." Julie's grin was even brighter thanks to her computer screen, and Ella couldn't help but match her.

"Wow, that's amazing! I haven't been great about staying in touch with him. You should talk to Rachel about having him move in here, we have the room. And I'll be gone basically until November."

Julie slammed her laptop shut. "Ella. That is BRILLIANT." She hopped off her stool, grabbing a couple wine glasses. "We should celebrate, it's five o'clock somewhere!" She bent over to pull the boxed wine from its pantry cupboard.

"Um, Julie?" Ella sighed. "I'm good. Gideon's coming over and I don't want to taste like… alcohol." She gave Julie a little smile.

"Oh my god, I'm so sorry. You're right." She put the supplies back. "Speaking of… drinking. How's Anthony?" She bit her lip, crossing her arms in front of her.

"Yeah, apparently Gideon and Tom visited him the other day. They say he's through the thirty day detox and is looking well. Keeping busy. I think he gets out next month." Ella watched her friend for any sign that betrayed how the news hit her.

Nothing.

"Oh, good. Glad to hear it." Julie opened the junk drawer, pulling out their stack of takeout menus. "Whaddya say we pick some options and order a feast later?" Her smile was full. Ella smiled back, hoping that her friend had truly been able to let go of the man who'd broken her heart.

"Yeah, that sounds great to me." Ella closed her laptop and picked up the Chinese food menu while Julie picked up the Thai. She would happily discuss food instead of work or boys until Gideon arrived.

48

Gideon looked down at the woman curled beside him, her breathing steady. His heart overflowed as it normally did when he gazed at Ella. Her backside was pressed against his front, her soft curves nestling against his hardened planes perfectly, the puzzle piece that had always belonged with him. His arm was nestled beneath the crook of her neck, and he tried to pull it out so as not to wake her. When he was successfully standing, the love of his life still breathing deep, he strode over to his pants he'd thrown on the floor by the window and found the box he'd kept there, waiting until the perfect moment.

He'd sat through a movie and a takeout feast with Ella and Julie. He'd sat through catching up with the two of them. He'd sat through another movie. He'd made it through a few rounds of filling her, melding their bodies until they were one, bringing her the ecstasy she deserved.

But he'd waited long enough.

The box was soft, heavy in his hand. Gideon opened it, the half carat diamond glinting in the moonlight. The fourteen karat gold band had been polished by a jeweler, resized thanks to Julie's help, and Gideon had added his own personal touch to the ring that held the heart of his parents. He'd had *As you wish.* engraved along the inside of the band, a nod to one of Ella's favorite movies. A nod to how far they'd come, and how far he would always be willing to go for her. He'd watched as many romantic movies as he could find, choosing the ones he knew Ella would love, and constructing the perfect proposal for her.

All he had to do was finish working up the courage.

Gideon took a deep breath and turned to face the bed. Ella's hair fanned out behind her, her bow lips parted. His angel. He knelt before her, resting an arm on the mattress in front of her, using his other hand to brush a stray lock of hair from her cheek. He brushed his knuckles down her exposed arm and her eyes fluttered open.

"Gideon?" Confusion wound itself across her forehead. She yawned, her hand rubbing her face. Gideon smiled, loving every move she made. He pulled out the box, watching her eyes go wide as he opened it.

"You had me at hello, Ella Davis. I didn't know how — or why — a woman could bewitch me the way you did, but I didn't question it. I opened myself up to the love and light you gave me. I don't know how — or why — an amazing, beautiful, strong woman would give me the chances that you did. You have always made me want to be a better man. I believe it was a million little things that meant we were supposed to be together. You have always felt like home. If you swoon, I'll catch you. If you want the moon, I'll pull it down. You should be kissed and often, and by someone who knows how. I don't know how to quit you, and when you realize you want to spend the rest of your life with somebody, you want the rest of your life to start as soon as possible. I love you. You complete me. Will you marry me, Ella Davis?"

It took every bone in his body to not wipe the tears falling from her eyes, her hand covering her mouth. He smiled when she nodded.

"Darlin', I need to hear you say it."

She laughed. "Yes! Yes, Gideon Pike, I want to marry you."

Gideon took her hand, sliding the ring in place before wrapping her in his arms, pulling her into a kiss he wanted to last forever.

He smiled, knowing that forever would never be enough for them to love each other, but it was a start.

Thanks so much for sharing Gideon and Ella's love story! If you enjoyed it, you'll love MORE THAN I SHOULD, Rebecca Stone's romantic and passionate new book.

Click here to order MORE THAN I SHOULD

Did you enjoy this book? Leave a review and let others know!

Find me online:

Facebook
Instagram
Website

Printed in Great Britain
by Amazon